GEMINI: RYDER

GEMINI DUET BOOK 1

THE SIN DEEP SERIES
BOOK 3

JODI PAYNE

BA TORTUGA

Gemini: Ryder
Copyright © 2026 by Jodi Payne & BA Tortuga

Edited by LC Hinson

Cover illustration by AJ Corza
http://www.seeingstatic.com/
Cover content is for illustrative purposes only and any person depicted on the cover is a model.

ISBN: 978-1-963644-21-0

Published by Tygerseye Publishing, LLC
April 2026
Printed in the USA

GEMINI: RYDER

Gemini: Ryder
A Sin Deep Novel
Jodi Payne and BA Tortuga

Widower Charles Martin has been very alone. His husband was lost to him long before Tad physically passed and Charles is at loose ends in their big, empty house. When a mutual friend suggests he hire a cowboy named Ryder as a personal assistant, he isn't sure what to expect.

Ryder Vales lost his bull riding career to a serious head injury that left him a different man. He's searching for something to do for work and for some peace in his life. He finds what he needs in taking care of Charles, serving and cooking for him, and in keeping him company.

Charles might be a good deal older than Ryder, but the two of them find comfort and then more together, building something that could seem odd to others, especially Ryder's twin brother Roper, but that makes them both happy. Ryder isn't sure if what he wants with Charles is what he deserves, though. Can Charles convince him that they're the only two people who need to care what their relationship looks like?

Gemini: Ryder is half of a duet!
The second book is titled Gemini: Roper
Ryder's twin brother's story.

The Sin Deep Series
Jodi Payne and BA Tortuga

Doms and Subs. Cowboys and city boys. Opposites attract, hurt-comfort, newbie subs and other romance tropes.

The Sin Deep Series is a collection of novels set in The Cowboy and the Dom Universe where Doms find their subs and subs discover themselves, their kinks, and a new kind of freedom.

Sin Deep

The Trouble with Cowboys

Gemini: Ryder

Gemini: Roper

As always, to our wives.

1

———————

"These are gorgeous, aren't they?" Charles tugged at the cuff of his husband's black silk pajamas. "Dolce and Gabbana. I knew you'd love them. Black suits you so well."

Although Tad hadn't been out in the sun for years and his skin wasn't tan anymore. In some places, it was actually translucent now. The deep black silk washed him out slightly, but it had always been Tad's favorite color, and it looked striking against the white sheets of the hospital bed.

"I had lunch with Brady; he sends his regards. We had champagne—you're jealous, right? I told him you would be." Brady was a good friend and their attorney. "Next month will be five years, Tad."

Five years was the limit. Five years and not a day more. The instructions in Tad's medical directive were very clear, and he had followed them to the letter, even when he felt like he couldn't anymore, or even shouldn't.

Brady had met with him to remind him that it was time, as if he'd needed reminding. It had been a long, difficult conversation after their initial toast, and he'd been glad for the little buzz the bubbles had given him.

But he was ready. He'd been ready for a long time.

"Good morning, sir. Ooh. Are those new pajamas? Spiffy."

He smiled at Jeremy, Tad's daytime nurse. "Do you like them?"

"I do." Jeremy felt the fabric and hummed appreciation. "Mm. They feel like heaven."

"I thought so. I hope he does too."

Jeremy hadn't brought it up yet, but he felt like something was in the air. Their five-year contract was ending soon and that knowledge sat like the proverbial elephant in the middle of the room.

Fortunately, Tad's room in their Lake George estate was very large.

"I—" Jeremy checked Tad's vitals, all the silent machines that kept him alive. "Is there anything you need, sir?"

"You're very kind, Jeremy. He hasn't got much time left, as you know, and I just want him to be comfortable and spoiled. I suppose that's ridiculous at this point."

"Of course not, sir." But Jeremy knew what he did. Tad was being kept alive by those machines now.

"Mm." Charles shrugged and wandered to the window. He'd chosen this room for Tad's hospital suite because of the huge windows and natural light, with its wide open view of the lake. It had been Tad's favorite view in the house. Really, it had always been Tad's room. It had been at one time Tad's home office.

"If you need me, please let me know. Would you like some tea?"

He would, in fact, but he wouldn't dream of asking Jeremy. Jeremy was here for Tad.

And pretty soon Jeremy wouldn't be here at all.

This house was going to be very big and lonely a month from now. Very big, and very lonely.

"Thank you, but I'll manage that for myself. You have work to do." Maybe he should hire someone as Brady had suggested, just so he wasn't knocking around this house alone. "I'll be heading back to the city shortly anyway."

"Yes, sir." He could tell that Jeremy didn't know what to say, so he simply left.

"I'll see you next weekend, darling." He kissed Tad's forehead and squeezed his hand, the ritual so familiar he hardly gave it a thought anymore.

He went straight to his office, skipping the tea, and picked up the business card Brady had given him at lunch. Was this what he wanted? Did he really want a stranger in his house, in his apartment in the city? Did he need a— what had Brady called it? A companion?

That word made him feel old. But then his husband dying so young at over a decade his junior made him feel old too. The thought of getting back out again as Brady had suggested—attending social events or worse, entertaining guests himself as he and Tad used to, shouldn't be so intimidating. It shouldn't make him so anxious, and yet it created such a feeling of dread, a heaviness in his chest that made it a little difficult to breathe.

Still, he probably should have someone to help him deal with the details—not for Tad, he would handle all of that himself with Brady's help—but for everything else.

Whatever "everything else" was.

A personal assistant. That was acceptable.

That was a call he could make.

2

———

R yder Vales checked his good button-down, shrugged on his best Western jacket, and grabbed his hat.

Tony said this was a good job—nothing too strenuous, nothing too dramatic. Just a widower who needed a handyman, a personal assistant, and a periodic arm candy moment at a function.

He had that handled.

Hell, he cooked too.

RYDER

Here. Wish me luck

It took about half a second for his other half to text back.

ROPER

Luck! U got this

He hoped so. He wanted a little peace and quiet.

The GPS had him headed for a lake house in the woods, and that seemed like exactly what the doctor ordered. Maybe he could do some fishing.

The winding road heading up to this place was wide and

paved, and the homes were enormous, which really wasn't what he thought of when he thought house by a lake, but he really had no idea where he was. Without Maps he'd be totally lost up here.

He'd told Rog he needed something away from his every day. Something less than normal. Somewhere he didn't have eyes on him all the time.

Rog promised this would do the trick.

Okay.

Okay, he could so do this.

Ryder slid out of his truck, his good boots clicking on the drive, and headed for the front door.

He rang the bell and waited.

And waited.

He looked around and found the number on one of the pillars on the front porch. He was in the right place. He reached forward to ring the bell again and the front door opened.

"Can I help you?" A silver-haired man stood in the doorway squinting at him with tired eyes.

"Yes, sir, I hope so. I'm Ryder Vales. I was hired by the Karmen Agency?"

"Oh. Uh. Yes, sorry. Of course. Come in." The guy looked a little confused but stepped out of his way and the door opened into a wide foyer that led to a living room with huge windows. "I'm Charles."

"Pleased to meet you." He took off his hat, held out his hand to shake. "How goes it?"

Charles seemed to compose himself then and shook his hand with a solid grip. "Good to meet you too. I apologize for my confusion. I don't meet too many men in cowboy hats. You weren't wearing one in the headshot in your dossier."

"No? I'm afraid they took about thirty thousand pictures in everything from bareheaded to a gimme cap to my Stetson." Why would that matter? He didn't follow.

"Well, it looks good on you." Charles looked uncomfortable again and ran one hand through his hair before looking at him. "I assume you're more experienced at this than I am. The kitchen is down that hall, your room is down there on the first floor. I'm upstairs." Charles looked around and nodded. "That's about it, I guess. My study is this way. I'll be in there. If you—um. That's where I'll be. Very good to meet you."

Charles turned around and disappeared down a hallway.

Okay.

He stood there a second, blinked a while, then went back out to his truck and called Rog. He had no idea what to do, or whether he needed to go or what.

Rog picked up immediately. "Just get out of your truck and go inside, man. You've got this."

How did he *do* that? "What am I supposed to do? He just left. Is there a manual?"

"He's a rich widower. What do you need to know? He's sad and lonely and probably hungry. Bring him tea, put his feet up, see if there's a banister that needs fixing, and make him some comfort food for dinner. Your mac and cheese or something. You know, be *you*."

"Okay. I just...it was like he wasn't expecting me. Am I supposed to try to talk to him or no?" He'd just expected questions or a manual or something.

"Ryder. He doesn't know you, and you don't know him. You're not going to walk in there and be all best buddies. It's been five minutes. Just play it by ear. And don't forget, man, this is a job. You're getting paid. You don't have to be friends;

you just have to make him happy enough that he wants to keep paying you."

"Okay." He didn't want to be friends. He just wanted to know whether or not to speak. He'd just not.

And Rog could fuck right off too.

He hung up without another word, grabbed his good shirts and his duffel bag, and shoved his phone in his pocket.

He went back inside, shut the door, and went to try to find a room "down there on the first floor" that looked as if it was for whatever he was.

Three meals and two snacks a day. Fix whatever he found that needed fixing. Stay in his room and read a lot. No talking.

He could do this.

He just needed to charge his earbuds.

His room was fancy. It had a king bed and its own bathroom with a big tub and a separate shower. There was a giant TV over the dresser with a nice sound bar and a comfy-looking chair and end table. The windows didn't look directly out over the lake, but he could see it and the woods were all green and lush.

He heard Charles clear his throat down the hall. "Sorry to bother you as you're just settling in, but do you plan to— is making dinner part of your job description, or do I need to arrange that for us?"

"Assuming you don't want anything involving live seafood or bugs, I'm happy to make you supper." He knew how to cook. "When would you like to eat, sir?"

He thought he heard a low chuckle and then Charles called back, "Seven, I guess?"

"I'll get on it." Mac and cheese with ham, if there was any.

He put his bag on the floor of the closet and put his good shirts on the rod.

RYDER

This isn't good. Also, blocking Rog on my phone.

ROPER

So leave. Is it creepy

He nodded, even though Roper couldn't see him.

RYDER

Just real quiet. No instructions. I guess I'll feed him and see what all needs fixin

ROPER

I miss u 2

RYDER

Yeah

Yeah, he wasn't used to being alone. Guess he'd start learning immediately and not bitch. He had a job. He'd just do it.

3

Charles finished off the last bite of the best macaroni and cheese he'd ever had, followed it with a sip of red wine that paired strangely well with it, and leaned back in his chair with a satisfied sigh. It had been a day full of unexpected things, which was refreshing after months of—*years* of knowing exactly how his days were going to go.

For starters, he hadn't expected a cowboy. That was an unimportant detail, but an interesting one. Something to wonder about, to occupy his thoughts for a while.

He hadn't expected to have dinner served for him, especially not such a delicious plate of soul-soothing comfort food.

And he hadn't expected to feel so relieved to know there was someone else in the house. Tad hadn't been much company, but he was someone to talk to. Even though Tad couldn't carry on a conversation, Charles had known he wasn't alone.

Lonely, but not alone.

He picked up his wine, dialed Brady on his cell phone,

and wandered over to the window to watch the last of the sunset.

"Charles. How are you?" Brady always sounded so pleased to hear from him.

"I am stuffed, my friend. A cowboy just fed me the best mac and cheese I've ever had, and I've called to thank you for that business card." He patted his belly. He'd eaten so much he felt like it might pop.

"A cowboy? As in yee-haw, y'all? Honestly?" Brady sounded as shocked as he'd felt when he saw the man walk up to the door in that hat and pointy-toed boots.

"Maybe not quite that stereotypical, but he was wearing lovely, expensive-looking, fancy boots. I probably insulted him with my own surprise." Ryder was well-dressed for the first day on the job. He was sure he owed the man an apology.

"He's there to keep you comfortable and taken care of. He'll be fine. Did he complain?"

Charles wasn't sure the man had spoken a dozen, polite, gentle words to him.

"No, not at all. He made a funny joke actually, about not cooking bugs when I asked him if making dinner was in his job description." Keep him comfortable and taken care of— that made it sound like he was helpless.

"Oh, that's good. That service is supposed to have incredibly well-rounded assistants."

"I'm not entirely sure I understand what I can and can't ask him to do, but I assume he'll tell me."

It occurred to him that in a perfect world, he wouldn't have to ask, the cowboy would just know. But it didn't work that way in reality, and he needed to figure out what he actually wanted from the man.

More macaroni and cheese would be a good start.

"Be honest and open, right? That's the most important part. I imagine he's just looking to make you happy."

He hadn't been the best at being open in his marriage. Honest yes, always. But totally open? He'd probably fail that litmus test.

He thought maybe it would be easier with a stranger, there was nothing to lose.

"That feels incongruous, being open with a man I don't know the first thing about."

"I imagine so, but I feel better knowing someone is there for you. Maybe he loves to watch TV or play cards or...uh... knit."

He snorted. "That would be something, if my personal assistant was a knitting cowboy." Cards were an idea. Maybe a whiskey. The cowboys on TV were always drinking whiskey. "I'll try, Brady. I'll...talk to him about...something."

He had nothing to lose in talking. Literally nothing.

"Go for it. There was a reason the service sent him. You had to be a good fit."

He didn't see it, but then again, he'd said three words to Ryder and got the world's best mac and cheese in return. So maybe there was something to it after all.

"You know this is difficult for me, Brady. I don't know how to be just me anymore. But I'll try."

"I do, and I'm proud of you, man. You're a survivor." He loved how Brady's voice rang with truth.

"Thanks. Let's do lunch in the city next week. Talk soon."

Brady shot him a calendar invitation as soon as they hung up the phone.

When he turned back to the table, he found his plate gone, and a piece of some sort of dessert with a scoop of ice cream on the side.

He glanced at it. Apple crisp, maybe? Or pear?

He couldn't remember the last time he'd had dessert. And look at that, he hadn't asked, it just happened.

But had Ryder overheard his conversation? That felt... awkward.

He sat and picked up the plate, which was warm underneath, and got a forkful of the fruit and some of the ice cream. It was warm and sweet, a bite of pure happiness.

He couldn't possibly finish it, he was still so full from dinner, but he ate more than half before he made himself put the plate down. It was apples, he wasn't sure if it was a crisp or a tart or what, but it was made from scratch for sure. How long had it been since he had a real, home-cooked meal?

Too damn long, obviously.

He wanted to say thank you, but he wasn't sure how to call for Ryder. He wasn't the shouting type, he didn't have a little bell or a buzzer. He moved to his desk and found Ryder's paperwork, and sure enough, there was a cell phone number.

But should he text or call?

He rolled his eyes at himself. It was ridiculous that even simple decisions made him anxious. He picked up his phone and dialed Ryder. He was a grown man, wasn't he? He could talk on the phone.

"Hello? Can I help you, sir?" The soft drawl was pleasant, not in the least harsh.

"Hi, Ryder. Could you come by my office, please? I thought we could—talk."

"No problem. I'll be there in two shakes."

"Very good. Thank you." He hung up, and before Ryder arrived he snuck one more bite of dessert. He was going to gain a hundred pounds if Ryder kept feeding him like this.

It didn't take but a few seconds for Ryder to knock on his office door. The man was in a white T-shirt, a pair of jeans with a kitchen towel in the back pocket, and a pair of boots that were less pointed and shiny as the ones he'd shown up in.

Also, the man's hair was completely silver, in a wild contrast to the unlined face.

He was a little jealous. His hair was also going silver, but his face showed the years around his eyes.

"Come in. Come sit." He waved Ryder over to a pair of comfortable leather wing chairs near the window. His view was of the back patio and the path down to the dock; it was shadier than the upstairs views but still had a nice look at the lake. "I really must apologize for my behavior when you arrived. I have reasons, but there was no excuse to be rude."

"No worries, sir." He got a nod and a half-grin. "This is my first time doing this, so I didn't understand the rules. I'm clever, though. I catch on quick."

He sat and gestured to the chair again. "Are there rules? Maybe you ought to explain to me what they are."

Ryder tilted his head, frowned. "Well, I suppose what you expect from me. When you want meals, what you like. What needs fixing..."

He nodded. "Dinner was outstanding. I don't think I've ever had macaroni and cheese that perfect. And the dessert was a lovely surprise. It made me smile. Thank you for that. As you can see, I was too full from dinner to finish it. Is that how you found this position? Are you a chef?"

"No, sir. I've worked in restaurants and as a camp cook a number of times, and I like cooking well enough, so I'm happy to do it."

He nodded. That was interesting. "Where are you from, Ryder?"

"Originally, New Mexico, although I've lived in Texas, Louisiana, and Colorado, and I've traveled all over."

Texas, New Mexico, Colorado...those places were definitely not like here. "So, why New York? I read your dossier; you could use your set of skills anywhere. From what I've seen so far, it seems like this is a new sort of position for you. I'm not questioning your competence, of course, I'm just curious what brought you up this way."

"It was time for a change of venue."

That was a nonanswer answer, but it weirdly didn't sound like a lie or even a prevarication.

He nodded his understanding. The details were none of his business if Ryder didn't care to share them. "Fair enough. I'm not looking for a change of venue, just a change of pace. I don't know what they've told you...?"

"Feed you, make you comfortable, take care of you."

That sounded exactly like what Brady had just said to him on the phone.

He was going to have talk with Brady about setting him up at lunch next week.

"That's what I've been told I need, yes." He sat up a little in his chair. "I've recently lost my husband." That was a strange and somewhat inaccurate thing to say because really, he'd lost most of Tad five years ago. But it was such a long story and Ryder didn't want to know all of that, he was sure.

Ryder nodded his head, almost bowing it. "I'm very sorry, sir. You got my sympathy."

"Thank you. I don't really know what's next for me, but I am told I should start doing things again. I have friends who are eager for me to accept the invitations I've been turning down for several years. They told you that I split my time between this house and the city?"

"Yes, sir. Rog explained to me that you'd need someone to attend functions with you as well. I know how to smile and nod for the public and for folks who you want to impress."

That made him grin. "You sound like you're a celebrity."

"No, sir, only in very certain circles that don't reach up here."

That explained Ryder's earlier statement—a change of venue. Ryder didn't want to be recognized. He was terribly curious, but he wasn't going to ask deeper questions of someone he barely knew. He wanted someone who understood the job, he didn't need a close relationship.

"So, is there a schedule you need me to follow? Likes? Dislikes?"

"I'll eat just about anything, so whatever you have on hand or feel like making is fine. I like a good breakfast, preferably with some fruit, and a latte or coffee with cream. I prefer a light lunch, salads and such, and dinners that fit the season. But otherwise, I'm pretty easy."

He thought about his schedule. "Here at the house, I have a relaxed schedule. Times don't matter so much as just going with the flow of the day. In the city I'm usually busier and I'll make sure you have my calendar."

"Of course." Ryder offered him a smile, and that was when he saw the scar that pulled at the corner of his lips. "That sounds good. Food allergies? Preferences?"

"No allergies. I love anything you'd put salsa on but not so spicy it makes me sweat. And I like sweets in small doses." Ryder was from New Mexico. The spicy warning seemed warranted.

"Yes, sir. I make basic stuff—tacos, enchiladas, mac and cheese, omelets—all the time, but I can follow a recipe just fine."

"I trust your judgment. And I hope—" He tried to be sincere but not overeager. "I hope you'll feel free to join me in the evenings if you have no other plans. Just to read, play cards, listen to music, that sort of thing."

"Of course. I'm good at all sorts of board games, cards— I've spent most of my adult life in hotel rooms, so I know how to be busy."

Piecing together all the little hints about Ryder's former life could easily become a hobby. "Do you have any more questions for me?"

"Do you have a list of repairs? Honey-dos? I've cleaned up the kitchen from dinner..."

"Honestly, I don't know." He'd spent all his time in his study or with Tad. "Maybe you can have a look around and let me know what you see. I've been...preoccupied in this house lately and haven't paid attention. It hasn't been a happy house for a long time."

"Not a problem. I'll get on it and give you a list of any supplies I need. What about groceries? How do you want me to work that?"

"You can just purchase whatever you need for supplies and groceries. I should have taken out stock in Uber Eats after Tad's accident. I never went shopping. I need coffee and cream daily, I like tea in the evenings, and everything else is up to you. There's a nice market in town, but nothing closer. It's a half an hour's drive or so. Please be sure to expense your mileage and fuel costs, and any supplies or tools you purchase."

"Yes, sir. I can do that. What kind of tea—iced, hot, sweet, lemon, green?" Ryder's fingers flew on his phone.

"Hot, decaf. You can mix it up, but I like black teas and fruity herbals. No sugar or milk, but sometimes I like honey. I'd just bring it every time in case." This was wild, having this specific conversation with Ryder about this, and he couldn't help but notice how Ryder seemed to relax more and more as they talked.

"Crispy bacon? Link or patty sausage? Biscuits or toast?" Those thumbs flew—he'd never seen anyone make notes so fast.

He watched, fascinated. "Crispy, please. I prefer links. Bread in all of its wonderful forms is fine by me. Toast, rolls, biscuits, scones, muffins…"

"Not a keto guy, then. Got it." There was that smile again, like it was hiding a secret.

"Definitely not. I don't eat large meals typically, but I like variety, and I don't diet." Typically. He'd just eaten his weight in macaroni. "What about you? Do you like to eat as much as you enjoy cooking?"

"I sure try to. I have to work to keep at my fighting weight." Ryder patted a perfectly flat belly.

Pretty. The cowboy must do a great deal of work. It was probably wrong that he wanted to see what was under Ryder's T-shirt, but he hadn't had thoughts like that in so long he didn't stop himself. He didn't stop himself from liking the way Ryder's dark eyes seemed to lighten up a little when he smiled. "Are you a boxer?"

"A boxer? Me? No, sir. I was a roughstock rider up until recent."

Roughstock. What was that exactly? "Like the rodeo?"

He got a firm, quick nod. "Yes, sir. Just like. I rode bulls."

Those pieces were falling into place. The scar, the celebrity status in certain places, those hard abs. "I'm afraid I don't know anything about rodeo, but it sounds like you must be pretty tough."

"I am. I was." Ryder gave him a wink. "Now I'm an old softy."

"You don't look soft to me." It wasn't until he heard himself say it that he thought perhaps he shouldn't have. "Objectively speaking, of course."

"Of course. So what else do you need me to know about you? So what else do you want from me?"

He gave that a second of thought, then shrugged. "I don't know. That seems like a good start. Let's just see how we work together shall we? I'll be headed back to the city Monday morning. You can ride in the car with me; there's nowhere to park your truck there. We'll stay until at least Thursday afternoon."

"Yes, sir. I've got three good shirts. I should be good to go." No matter what he said, it was like water off a duck's back.

He started to say that Ryder wasn't going to have to dress, but he didn't actually know. He had a dinner Wednesday evening, and he really didn't know what else might be going on.

"Don't worry, sir. I won't embarrass you. You got my word."

"Oh. I'm not worried about that, Ryder. Not at all." Well, maybe a little. He knew a cowboy on his arm would raise a few eyebrows. He just wasn't sure he cared.

"Well, I have been told I can talk to trees, so it should work out."

He chuckled. "You may find yourself in your element, then." The room went quiet for a moment, and he decided that rather than invent small talk, they should end on a high note. He stood. "Thank you for everything."

Ryder stood as well, offered him a hand. "You're more than welcome. Holler if you need me. I'll have breakfast ready when you need it."

"Thank you. You don't mind if I text? You can certainly

text or call if you need me as well." Ryder didn't seem like he needed much from him, though.

"Of course I don't mind. Text away. I'm right down the hall."

"I'm headed upstairs in a minute. Goodnight, Ryder. Thanks again."

Ryder picked up his empty tea mug and the plate of dessert, saying goodnight before he left the room.

What an interesting young man.

He certainly had a lot to think about. He thought he'd made up for his curt greeting this afternoon, and it seemed like Ryder was very happy to have some marching orders. What tomorrow would be like he couldn't say, but he felt like he might sleep better tonight knowing Ryder was just a few steps away.

4

———————

Ryder had cleaned out the fridge, had washed and pressed his shirts and jeans, and polished his boots.

His electronics were charged, and he was ready to be "in the city".

See him. See him learning new things.

Like was he supposed to talk to Charles on the drive or sleep or listen to his headphones...

He glanced up at the clacking sound of men's dress shoes on the hardwood floors. Charles was headed his way wearing a flawlessly tailored blue dress suit, striped tie and carrying a briefcase.

"We'll need a couple of bottles of water for the drive," Charles said, setting his briefcase down in the foyer and tugging on his cuffs.

"Yes, sir." He'd grabbed the little Yeti cooler from his truck, and he held it up. It had six bottles of water, some cheese and grapes, and two Dr Pepper Zeros.

Charles peered out the window as if he was making sure the car was here, which it was. It had arrived early this morning and had been parked out there ever since. "Ready then?" Charles gave him a smile. "Don't forget your hat."

"No, sir. I don't go anywhere without one." He had a dove gray felt 10X that made him feel amazing.

"I'd assumed as much. Lock up, please." Charles put a coat over one arm and picked up his briefcase, then made his way out to the car.

He made sure he had his book, grabbed his shirts, the cooler, and his bag, then locked the door. This wasn't hard work, and he could easily get used to being at the house—there was plenty to do with minor repairs, futzing around to make things nice.

Now he'd figure this part out.

He had music playing softly in his one earbud. It made it easy to hear his phone notifications and not bother Mister Charlie.

They climbed into the wide, cushy backseat of a black sedan and Charles got comfortable. "Good morning, Alan. This is Ryder, my new assistant."

Alan gave him a quiet nod in the rearview. "Straight to the apartment, sir?"

"I think so. Do we need to stop anywhere, Ryder?"

"No, sir." Where would they stop? He'd been to New York City once, when he'd thought he'd be a big-time bull rider. It hadn't lasted.

At all.

He remembered landing at the airport, waking up in the hospital, and Roper coming to fetch him home after the brain swelling had gone down. All in all, he'd lost ten days.

"Straight to the apartment then, Alan. Thank you."

"Yes, sir." The car was warm and cozy and the ride was smooth as they headed down the winding mountain road.

"I bought the lake house a couple of years before I met

Tad. He loved this drive. He'd point out the same things along the way, things that he liked such as this big tree coming up with huge winding branches—that one right there." Charles pointed as they drove by. "And there is a house up here with these ridiculous statues out front."

Ryder thought they were kind of cool—not as cool as a huge iron buffalo but cool nonetheless.

Charles glanced at him, and he realized that the small talk about the statues was just a way of getting the conversation started. "I understand if you don't wish to talk about it, so please don't hesitate to tell me if I'm overstepping, but I'm so curious about your riding career. Did you ride for a long time?"

He turned to face Charles and smiled. This was part of the job he understood. "I did, especially for a roughstock guy. I started at fifteen, got my card at eighteen, and rode for ten years."

"Your card is for a professional membership? Or a license?"

"It's the PRCA card—Professional Rodeo Cowboy Association. You pay your dues in, and you're a member, then you can ride in sanctioned rodeos." He remembered saving for that first set of cards—him and Roper had worked all summer, heads down, doing anything and everything to pay their dues.

"Ten years seems like a long time for such a dangerous sport. So you're retired now?" Charles was asking questions kindly and seemed to be genuinely curious.

"Yes, sir. I had a career-ending injury." He remembered when Roper told him.

Bubba, it's over. You cain't jostle your brain no more. Doc says so.

"Oh, I'm sorry. That must have been difficult to swallow."

"It's the nature of the beast." And he wasn't going to whine about it, but he'd lost more than anyone except Roper might understand. Still, that wasn't none of Mister Charlie's. Not at all. "It's a young man's game."

"Mm. I know a little something about that." Charles pointed to his silvery hair. "Although yours doesn't seem to have anything to do with age."

"No, sir. We started going gray at sixteen, and we're all the way gone by the time we graduated high school."

"We?" Charles looked confused. "Oh. Sister? Brother?"

"My brother. Roper." His best friend. The son of a bitch who made him angrier than anyone. His twin.

"Where is he? New Mexico?"

"Right now?" He pondered that. "He's in Anaheim. He'll be in Oakland Thursday."

"He's still riding." Charles nodded like he was putting pieces together. "You'll have to tell me if his tour brings him out this way at all. I've never been to a rodeo."

"It does, now and again. In fact, my career ended in New York City." Go team him.

"Well, I hope you won't hold it against her." Charles smiled at him. "Maybe you'll make some new, better memories for yourself. Which reminds me, we haven't talked at all about days off. What are your thoughts?"

He hadn't really put his mind to it, but what was he going to do? "I don't know, to be honest. What works for you?"

"Well, I think you should have one day a week, or the equivalent, so you could pick a steady day, pick a day based on what the next week looks like, or add them together and take a few days off a month. It's really up to you. Paid days, of course."

"I—Sure. Totally." Was he supposed to leave on his days

off? He could save up like four days a month and fly to see Roper, he guessed. Lord knew he had airline miles.

"I'm flexible. You can do whatever you like, just be sure I have some notice. Fair?" Charles pulled out his phone and looked at it, scrolling slowly.

"Of course. I'm pretty easy." And not sure what usually happened in these situations.

He wasn't going to call Rog, though.

No way.

He'd just figure everything out by his damn self.

"You do seem fairly relaxed, it's true." Charles seemed to approve.

It was a four-hour drive to New York, and they couldn't talk the whole way, right? Charles put on headphones and disappeared into his phone for a while, and Alan never said a word after they left the driveway.

So, he texted Roper.

RYDER

heading to NYC

ROPER

fun fun. Doing anything cool

RYDER

dunno. Just going to be…friendly? it's not a hotel, it's an apartment. I'll cook for sure. Make coffee

ROPER

housewife

RYDER

yep. Hes nice tho. Quiet. Busy. I basically make coffee and tea and look hot

ROPER

asshole. I'm hotter

RYDER

always, but I'm better hung

ROPER

I'm sure Mr. NYC would love to know that

RYDER

No way. He's in mourning. It's sad. Just lost his guy. Married & everything

ROPER

WHOA

RYDER

inorite? :(

ROPER

is he hot too? tell me he's hot. I'm so sick of looking at cowboy butts

There was a pause and then Roper added,

that's a lie, I will never get sick of cowboy butts

He fought his chuckle.

RYDER

super pretty, in a sad, serious SUPER CLASSY way. He's like a model.

ROPER

Oh, so you're fucked. You draw rednecks

RYDER

like moths to a bug zapper

ROPER

use your personal fund to pay them to go away. you have one right? a fund? I think that's a rich people thing.

He rolled his eyes.

RYDER

U do remember the $2.5mil medical bill?
Bankruptcy? I got a laptop, a truck, & a
phone.

ROPER

Right…you got a sexy bro too

RYDER

I know. You look JUST LIKE ME. Lucky you!

ROPER

Funny. Less beat up.

Yeah, but with a beard and longer hair, no one would tell them apart.

RYDER

Give it time butthead

ROPER

so is this an I need to talk to Ro text convo
or an I am avoiding texting Rog convo? he
says ur not answering his texts. U rly
blocked him?

RYDER

he said to deal w shit on my own. I have my
dealing hat on

Roper would understand that. Rog wouldn't have given him this job if Roper hadn't been in his back pocket.

ROPER

ooh that's a nice hat. Brand new and barely
worn!

RYDER

Like you know about the hat. Fucker.

ROPER

Don't make me send you a dick pic

RYDER

EEEEEEEEW

Gross.

ROPER

You're good, bro. Promise. This shit is right
in your wheelhouse. Cooking, fixing shit,
taking care. So you.

RYDER

Yeah. He's a sweet guy. Quiet.

Ryder thought he was just in need of someone in the house so he wasn't alone. That was fair.

"Skyline." Charles pointed out the window. "Beautiful today in this clear weather. Won't be long now."

"Oh, that's pretty." Big. It was pretty cool, actually. He took a quick picture and sent it to Roper.

ROPER

Wow. Ur really there. That's pretty

RYDER

I am. It is. ttyl. Love you

He needed to be social and friendly and all.

ROPER

ditto

"Are you hungry?" Charles put his phone away too. "We could put our things down and go get some lunch before we settle in."

"I could totally eat. Also, I have grapes and cheddar, just

in case you get peckish." He was good at dealing with peckish folks. Roper was a turd when he was hangry.

Charles seemed pleased and gave him a kind smile. "Oh, I'd love a snack. What a great idea. We still have the bridge traffic to get through."

"I have extra sharp and just plain old sharp, plus red and green grapes." He was an extra-sharp cheddar guy, himself.

He pulled out the Tupperware containers with the food, opening them up, easy peasy.

"Extra sharp please, though honestly, it's cheese. I'm afraid I have little willpower." And as if to prove it, Charles reached right in and took two slices. "I think I'm more of a green grape person, though red grapes are sweeter. I suppose it's good that I don't have to choose."

"There you go. I just go for no seeds. Grape seeds are no fun at all." They got in his teeth.

"Seedless is preferable," Charles agreed. They both reached into the little tub of grapes at the same time and their fingers tangled. Charles chuckled but didn't yank his hand away. "Terribly sorry."

He chuckled. "You first. It's only fair."

Charles was the boss, after all, and they were his grapes.

"Green for me, then." Charles plucked a couple out of the container and popped them in his mouth. "Mm. Is there a better combination than grapes and cheese?"

"Olives and cheese." That was his absolute favorite. "I do love me some olives."

"Mm. Also good. Nice and salty." Charles reached for a bottle of water and opened it, then took a big gulp.

"Yeah. I'll add olives next time. They can be polarizing."

Charles chuckled. "Such a diplomatic way of putting it."

"That's me. Diplomats R us." He tickled himself, honest to God. "So are you a green or a black olive guy?"

"Black on pizza, green as a snack. Is there any other way?" Charles winked at him. "I'm not a pimento fan, however."

"No? I love pimento cheese." And green olive and pepperoni pizza was his absolute favorite.

"You may have all of my pimentos. Pimento? What's the plural? I have no idea."

"Pimentos, I guess. Although I've heard folks pronounce them pim-i-entos."

"Fancy." Charles peered out the window. "Are we over the bridge already, Alan?"

"Yes, sir. I'll have you home in a few minutes."

"You're a good distraction, Ryder. Or maybe it's the cheese."

"Maybe it's the grapes," he teased. "It could happen."

Charles just rolled his eyes.

5

———

Charles finished checking his emails and got up from his desk to stretch his legs. He often felt stiff after the drive from Lake George, but he'd taken Ryder on a walk around his neighborhood after lunch, which had been a good stretch of the legs, and he was feeling great.

Ryder seemed to enjoy his favorite local pizza establishment, and it was a gorgeous fall day with plenty of sunshine, so he'd drawn out his little tour to include a few of the places Ryder might have reason to visit—the grocery, the pharmacy, his favorite flower shop, the bagel shop, his dry cleaner. Unlike at the lake where everything they needed was a drive, here in the city all of those things were within easy walking distance.

Ryder appreciated the walk and even took notes in his phone as he often did when he wanted to remember something. Charles understood that his attention was simply so Ryder could do his job well, but it was comforting to feel like the things he cared about were important to someone again. Even if that someone was a paid staff member.

He found Ryder staring out the window, earbuds in, dancing to whatever music was playing. From the back, without the hat on, Charles could see a pattern of scars that the silver hair couldn't quite hide.

Easy enough to assume that career-ending injury had been a head injury, and he had to believe that Ryder was lucky to be alive and with his wits about him.

"That's another decent view, right?" From that window, Ryder could see the top half of the tall Midtown buildings and the trees in Central Park. And it was a great view of the blue sky that was hard to get from just anywhere.

Ryder glanced at him, smiled and nodded. "It's real cool. I took a bunch of pictures. You have an idea what you want me to make you for supper tonight?"

"Something light. I'm still full from that pizza. Maybe a salad?" He stepped in beside Ryder to take in the view as well. "There's a rooftop garden. If you ever want to take a break, it's a lovely spot. Just take the elevator up to the top floor and follow the signs to the roof door."

"Okay. That would be cool. I'll have to go explore." Ryder smelled like Ivory soap, and it made him smile. He'd had Ivory soap in the bath when he was a boy. "Do you have a schedule here that's different than at...home? Is this home? Or just the lake and here?"

That was a good question, which place he considered home. He'd been splitting his time for so long it was more habit than choice. "The lake and here...for now." He was going to give that some thought. "My schedule here is busier. I just emailed you a link to my calendar a few minutes ago. That seemed to make more sense than having to tell you day to day. Tonight is quiet. Tomorrow, I have some calls in the morning and a board meeting in the afternoon, and then I expect I'll have a dinner invitation after the board meeting. If so, I'd like you to join me."

"Of course. You just say whether you want me to wear the white, gray, or black shirt." Ryder pulled his phone back out and grabbed his email, opening his calendar.

He'd never have guessed a rodeo cowboy would be so tech-savvy.

"Well, let's see what the invitation is." He did like the idea of bringing a cowboy to dinner. They'd turn a few heads, and he felt as if Ryder would be able to hold his own. "Black for sushi, white for Italian, and gray if we're going to someone's home?" That made him chuckle. As if there were a formula for such things.

"Only if I don't eat spaghetti. Red sauce and white is a dangerous combo."

"I might just make you wear it now on a dare." He smiled, feeling a little daring himself.

"I'll be in mourning for my shirt. Poor my shirt!"

Charles laughed gently, and the sound was a little awkward in his ears. It had been a while. "Poor your shirt? I'll buy you two more."

"Maybe they'll have big bibs that I can tie behind my neck." Ryder was playing with him. Teasing him.

He glanced at Ryder, then back out the window. "Oh, I'm sure. They have hobby horses and little cowboy hats and baby blue lassos on them."

"Those are my favorite!" Those near-black eyes went wide.

"Ha!" He laughed in earnest this time, he couldn't help himself. "Your point, cowboy."

Ryder bowed for him, and that laugh warmed him, all through.

"All right, clever cowboy. I would like some tea, please. Something with caffeine." He had some reading to do before his meeting tomorrow.

"Yes, sir. I got your back." Ryder went to the kitchen, and Charles could hear the water running and soft singing starting up.

He enjoyed Ryder's singing. He'd heard it every so often at the lake house, too, and it relaxed him for some reason. He felt like Ryder was comfortable in his space, and that made him feel good.

He took a seat on the couch and picked up his iPad to look over some documents, which wasn't at all what he wanted to do. He wanted to keep talking with Ryder. He wanted to ask questions that were none of his business.

He wanted to just...enjoy the company. Ryder was warm, clever, funny. An all-around decent guy, at least so far.

"Ryder," he said as soon as Ryder appeared with his tea. "I'd like to take you up to the roof after dark so you can see the skyline all lit up. What do you think?"

"That sounds amazing. I'd love that, if you don't mind." Ryder didn't sound like he was faking it.

"Not at all; it's one of my favorite things to do here, and with a clear day like today it should be spectacular." And it gave him an excuse to have Ryder's company.

"Are you a tea drinker?" He felt that was a fair question, not too personal.

"Iced tea, mostly. I'm learning about hot tea. I didn't have any idea how many different versions of tea there are."

"Mm. Yes. There is something for just about every taste. I find it relaxing, a warm drink. You should try a green tea. I believe you'd like it."

"A green tea—you make the water less hot and brew for a shorter time."

He blinked at Ryder. "You researched tea?"

"Yes, sir. You drink it."

He gave Ryder a gentle smile and a short nod. "I appreciate that." There was something remarkable about Ryder, the way he'd taken this role on, making it more than a job in just a few short days.

Ryder nodded once, smiled. "It's important to take care."

He understood that. He'd been looking after Tad for years even though it didn't come naturally to him. It was just what you did for people you loved. People you cared about. Maybe it was his turn now. Not that he could have anticipated someone like Ryder.

"Are you sure you've never done this before?"

"Done what? I mean… I've always been with Roper, so I've always had someone close to take care of, I suppose."

"I meant worked for an agency like this, but I see your point. No wonder you're so good at this if you've always looked after him."

"It's…" Ryder looked a little confused for a moment. "I'm glad that I accepted the position."

He nodded in complete agreement. "Me too. So. I need to get a look at this agenda and some documents for my meeting tomorrow, but then let's have an early dinner, and we'll visit the roof for sunset."

"Yes, sir. Salad and maybe some garlic knots. I'm on it." Ryder smiled at him again. "Holler if you need me."

He didn't "holler"; that wasn't his style, but of course he understood what Ryder meant. "I'll text. Thank you." He did like garlic though.

He couldn't explain it, but he felt as if Ryder had been there forever instead of a handful of days. He missed Tad's company, but he was used to that; he'd missed it for many years. Ryder was a different kind of company. One he found he appreciated at this point in his life. Their rapport was already so easy, friendly even. Ryder just fit right into his space, quietly and perfectly.

He picked up his tea and sipped it, curious suddenly about how long one steeped a nice decaf black tea.

He'd have to ask Ryder.

6

Ryder put on one of his good shirts, his best jeans, and his good boots. He had a gray Western jacket that matched his hat, and his buckle from when he won Austin.

He was looking *good*.

He wasn't sure exactly what "dinner at the penthouse" meant, but it sounded swanky.

All he had to do was smile and look pretty. No arguing. No opinions. No nonsense. Hold Mister Charlie's chair out for him.

Be a gentleman.

"Ryder, can you give me a hand here?" Charles came down the hall in a navy suit and a blue and yellow tie, fussing with a cufflink. "I haven't worn these in forever, and now I recall why. They're a bear to get on by myself."

"Of course. Hold up." He sat his hat down, brim up, and set himself to helping. "You look lovely."

Charles held an arm out, then froze, eyes looking him up and down. "Ryder, you look incredible. That jacket is perfect on you. So well-tailored too."

Oh, that was nice to hear. "Thank you, sir. It's my favorite."

"I can certainly see why. You're going to turn heads at dinner, I hope you won't mind the attention."

"I'll be sweet as Tupelo honey, sir, you got my word." He fastened the first cuff, then went for the second.

"Ah, thank you. I can't tell you how long I was fumbling with these before I remembered I have you to ask." Charles smiled at him. "It's been a while since I dressed for dinner. Meetings, sure, but a night out? I can hardly remember the last time."

"So is there anything I need to know? I mean beyond the no religion, no politics, no sex talk part."

"Actually, those are all fair game. Money is a good subject to avoid with this group, the stock market, and possibly family."

He knew a lot about stock—stock tanks, livestock, stock farmers... "I doubt that's going to be a problem."

Charles chuckled. "I'm not a stock market man either. I have a guy who does that for me. We're going to do just fine together."

"Yes, sir." He winked at Charles. "All good to go."

In fact, Charles was quite handsome. More than good to go.

Charles fussed with his tie, resettled his jacket on his shoulder, and leaned over and swiped at his dress shoes. "Well, I suppose I have no excuse to procrastinate any longer."

"It'll go fast." He wasn't sure why Charles was dreading this, but it would go quick.

"I'm sure it'll be a lovely evening; it just feels foreign to me now. I haven't been social like this for a few years." Charles offered him an arm. "Shall we try it out?"

"Yes, sir. I am at your disposal." He took Mister Charlie's arm. "Let's do this thing."

"To the car, then."

The ride didn't take very long. They stopped outside a tall, shiny building with lots of windows no one could see into and a lobby full of marble and elevators.

"Car six I think he said."

"Pardon me?" What car? Did they need to go back outside?

"Car six goes to the penthouse." Charles looked at him, then grinned. "Oh. Fancy word for an elevator. Only used in fancy buildings."

"Ah. Good to know. I was fixin' to walk you back outside." Lord have mercy. Elevator car sounded weirdly familiar—maybe from his granny? His pappy?

"My apologies. Victor calls it a car, so I did the same." Charles was smiling now, though, and seemed more relaxed.

The *car* went up and up, finally stopping just before his ears popped. The doors opened into a bright foyer, and they were approached by men in black tailcoats and bow ties. One of them held out a white-gloved hand, palm up toward him. "May I take your hat, sir?"

"That's all right. I'll keep ahold of it, if you don't mind." He didn't imagine these folks knew it, but this hat cost twice what he paid for his iPhone.

Charles nodded to him in approval and offered his arm again. "It's more than just a hat," he told the man and the butler stepped back again, gesturing for them to move inside.

"Yessir. It's *my* hat." He appreciated Mister Charlie's understanding. He knew not everyone did. He squeezed Charles's arm. "Thank you."

"My pleasure. Purely selfish motives, I'm afraid. It looks so good on you." Charles gave him a playful wink.

"Charles!" A tall, blond man in a light gray suit hurried over. "I was so happy to hear that you'd accepted my invitation. What a wonderful surprise."

"Victor. I may have surprised myself too, but it's time. Past it." They shook hands, and Charles gestured to him. "Victor Weber, this is Ryder Vales."

Victor gave Charles a quick smile, then looked Ryder in the eye. "A pleasure. Welcome to my home."

"Pleasure is all mine, sir. Thank you." He knew all about how to be polite, and these folks were obviously tickled that Charles had come out of mourning.

"Come in. Say hello and have a drink." Victor led them toward a small bar, but it took ages to actually get there. They were greeted along the way by everyone they passed. He had no hope of remembering all the names.

That wasn't really his job, he supposed. He was meant to nod, smile, and take care of Charles. The rest was just details.

"Charles! Is that really you?"

Charles turned at the sound of the big voice and laughed. "River!"

"It's so good to see your face!" The big man hugged Charles tight, almost picking him up off the ground.

"Thank you. I'm sure it would be lovely to see yours but you're squeezing me too tight." Charles was smiling as River let him go.

"You look spectacular. I hope you got my note."

"Yes, thank you. I appreciate the kind things you said about Tad."

"He has been and will be missed, but I'm happy to see you out and about again."

"Thank you. River, this is Ryder."

River's eyebrow went up. "Ryder. Good to meet you. You look familiar for some reason."

A guy popped up next to River's arm like a jack-in-the-box. "Probably the hat. We all look the same in them, you know. I'm Kacey."

River snorted, eyes rolling fondly.

Oh, this man was something else, he could tell. He held out one hand. "Pleased."

River shook his hand and smiled at him. "Welcome to New York. It's not for everyone, but you're in good hands."

"Thank you, sir." He had no idea what River meant, but smiling and nodding was the rule of the night.

"What are you drinking, Ryder? Vic literally has everything." Kacey elbowed him.

He glanced at Mister Charlie. He didn't know if that was cool or not, to have a beer. He was technically on the clock...

Charles gave him a nod. "Kacey isn't exaggerating. Have whatever you can dream up. I'll have a gin and tonic, please."

He let Kacey lead him to the bar, but he knew River and Charles were talking about him as soon as they stepped away. River glanced at him more than once, and with interest.

He wasn't going to gossip, but he didn't want to seem mean, either, so he let Kacey lead the conversation. He could nurse a beer all evening long.

"It's nice to see Charles out with someone. He's a good man. Did you meet in the city or out at the lake?"

"At the lake." *I'm the hired pretty. Like a personal assistant slash companion.*

"Well, I hope it works out. He took very good care of Tad,

from what I hear. I didn't know the guy though. You want a beer?"

"Please." Mister Charlie rarely spoke about his husband, but what he'd gathered, the man had been ill for a long time.

Kacey asked for two beers, the gin and tonic for Charlie and a rum and Coke, he had to assume was for River. "I think I remember that Charles likes extra lime," Kacey suggested with a wink. "In case you want brownie points."

"I don't think that's an option, but if it makes him happy, then I'll bring more limes."

"Brownie points aren't an option?" Kacey chuckled. "Bummer."

He winked, chuckling softly. That wasn't in the job description. "I'm *so* abused."

Kacey grinned and handed over Charles's drink and his beer. "Yeah. I can see you have it rough. There's a secret back elevator if you need to escape. I'll cover you."

"I think I'll risk it, but thanks." He liked this guy. He had a sense of humor. "And thank you for the drinks."

"Hey, the arm candy has to stick together." Kacey led the way back to Charles and River.

"Ah, look who's back. Oh, and extra lime. Thank you, Ryder." Charles took his drink and sipped it right away.

"Yes, sir. You're welcome." He took a tiny sip of his beer. "You holler if you want another."

"I will do that." Charles smiled at him.

"Charles, it was good talking with you. Let's catch up again. I'll call you."

"I would like that."

"Welcome back."

"Thank you very much." Charles nodded to River, and

Kacey gave him a little finger wave and a grin as they moved off farther into the penthouse.

Charles touched his shoulder. "This is a good drink. I haven't had one in a while. How is your beer?"

He felt that touch deep in his bones, somehow. Weird. "Nice and hoppy, thank you."

Charles offered an arm again. "Care to wander a little? Victor has an amazing home."

"I'd love that, thank you. Are you friends? Colleagues?" He took Mister Charlie's arm and stepped close.

"Victor and I served on a board together a few years ago. We travel in the same circles now. We're both investors."

"That's cool. Everyone here is obviously glad to see you."

Charles smiled but there was something a little sad about it. "It's a little surprising. Tad was so much better at social gatherings than I am. It's nice to think that I was missed."

Oh, poor guy. Ryder just wanted to hug him. It must be hard to miss his guy. "Well, obviously you're well-liked."

"Yes, perhaps. I do hope that's true. I suppose that's what we're doing these social events for, right? To find out, to maybe make some new connections, reestablish some old ones."

"There you go." Eventually Charles would find himself a sweetheart, and he'd be hanging out at the house and listening to an audiobook.

Maybe he'd be fired when that happened.

Who knew?

Charles leaned a little closer as they walked. "River thought we made a good couple. I didn't know what to say, so I just said thank you."

"That's fine. They can think whatever you want them to."

He didn't mind. He was here to make Mister Charlie's life easier.

"Charles." The way the blond-haired man said Charles's name was odd. "Look at you. You're looking well."

Charles raised an eyebrow. "Lewis. You're looking just the same."

"Thank you."

He didn't think Charles had meant that as a compliment.

"How have you been? I see you've found yourself a little cowboy. He's adorable."

"It's been a difficult month, as I am sure you know. Lewis," Charles tone was terse. "This is Ryder. He was a rodeo cowboy until recently, and I am very sure he could kick your ass."

"Goodness, such language. You have changed. What would Tad say?"

"Oh, Tad would definitely cheer him on."

"Honestly. Still such a bear. I'm ready to buy that lake house."

"My estate is not for sale."

"Tad's estate, you mean. And it really ought to be mine."

"Lewis, we need to move on. I'd like to say it's been a pleasure, but it never has. Excuse us." Charles steered them right around Lewis, who laughed as they left, but it didn't quite land as the man had probably intended.

"What an asshole. I could take him downstairs and clean his clock if you'd like me to, sir." He knew Charles would probably say no, but he had to offer. It was the kind thing to do.

Charles put an arm around his shoulders. "Thank you, Ryder. Just knowing that you could is more than enough for me."

"Any time." He chuckled softly. "So, tell me, what's your favorite part of this house?"

They'd played this game every place Mister Charlie had taken him.

"Oh, the balcony. You have to see the balcony." Charles steered them, with that arm still around him, toward a wall of glass windows. It was impossible to see out of them with how bright the room was, but a set of double doors was open at one end, and Charles led him through to a wide balcony with a glass railing and a view of a busy street with tons of lights and flashing signs. "Midtown. That's Times Square."

"Oh, wow. Wow, that's beautiful." He snapped a couple of pics. Roper would love that.

"See the river? That's the Hudson, and then the bridge beyond goes to New Jersey. If you squint, you can see the statue of Liberty right...there." Charles pointed out into the darkness.

His lips parted, and he leaned to look. "Oh, look at that."

"So, this is my favorite part of this house. What's yours?"

"This is amazing. Absolutely stunning. Thank you, sir. This is beautiful." He didn't have enough words for pretty.

"How about that? We agree on the best part. That's a first." Charles looked out over the city and Ryder could tell Charles really did enjoy the view by the look of wonder on the man's face. "This just never gets old."

"Is this home for you?" They'd never really discussed that.

"You mean where am I from, hm? Well, I was born in Los Angeles and was there until my parents divorced, then I relocated to upstate New York with my father. I stayed with him until I left for college, and I fully intended to never be associated with him again, but—" Charles turned and leaned against the railing, the look on his face part amusement and part confusion. "Somehow, in her attempt to murder my father, his fourth wife accidentally blew up their vacation yacht while she was still on it, and I inherited everything." Charles's lips curled into a grin. "And everything turned out to be quite a bit more than I had imagined."

"Are you shitting me? That's a story and a half!" His was way simpler, when it came right down to it. He was a twin. They had a pair of twin brothers. Momma and Daddy were rodeo people, so were all of them.

Charles laughed softly. "No one ever believes me, but it's the absolute truth. Including the murder. She had done all the research on her laptop and even kept the receipts for her purchases. I'm not sure what she thought she was going to do with them—write them off her taxes? The entire probate hearing was morbidly hilarious. As it turned out, in an ironic twist, she needn't have bothered to go to all the trouble. He'd left everything to me, including the yacht she destroyed."

"Was it insured at least?" The words just popped out of his mouth.

Charles laughed. "Oh, it was, but it was all null and void because she blew the damn thing up on purpose."

"Lord have mercy! Well, I tell you what, you have had a fascinating damn life." Not easy, it sounded like, but interesting.

"Hm." Charles sobered a bit. "Fascinating is one way to put it. For all that was amusing, I don't care to relive it."

"Oh, no. Of course not! That's not what I meant at all." Lord have mercy, he needed to keep in mind that he wasn't a goddamn friend or a lover or even a dude that Charles wanted to hang with. He was hired, sight unseen, by his twin's old lover, and he needed to stop having thoughts or opinions out loud.

Charles patted his arm. "I know, Ryder. Don't worry about it. It is a funny story, and I offered it as such. You're just fine. Should we take in the rest of the penthouse?"

"Yes, sir. Sounds great." He found a smile, even though there was a little ache in the pit of his belly. "Lead the way."

7

———————

Charles stumbled off the elevator feeling a little embarrassed by how much he'd had to drink. He hadn't been drunk enough to feel it in years and, apparently, his current tolerance for gin and tonics was no longer what it used to be.

"I'm sorry," he said as Ryder caught his elbow. Had he been falling? He hadn't felt like he was falling. "This is very embarrassing. I never do this. I'm so sorry."

His skin didn't feel as thick as it had once been either. Perhaps that was more of the issue. Running into Lewis had surprised him when he really should have been prepared. "Lewis is Tad's ex, you know. Lewis thinks because I gave the lake house to Tad that I should sell it now that he's gone. He's made four offers. I keep having to ask my lawyer to turn him down."

The words sounded perfectly clear in his head, but he wouldn't have been surprised if they sounded like drunken ravings on Ryder's end. "I don't get drunk at these things all the time, I promise. This is so humiliating."

"Why? You're not puking or driving. You're fine, just

feeling good. We're going to get in the car, have some water. Also, that Lewis guy is a little prick."

He nodded. Lewis was a prick. That was the perfect thing to say. Ryder was very good at that. "You are right. A prick. And water." He nodded again. "Really. This is not in your job description."

"I know, but that's okay. Not everything needs to be, right? We'll just say I'm off the clock right now, huh?"

"You're very kind, Ryder. I am growing quite fond of you." He probably wouldn't have said that if he were sober, but he wasn't, and he thought it was okay. He let Ryder help him into the car and rolled his eyes when Ryder even put a hand on his head so he didn't hit it getting in.

He'd needed it, too, which made him giggle like an idiot. God, he was a mess.

"Listen to you. You might oughta have a sip or two a little bit more often. It's probably good for your stress levels." Ryder didn't sound like he was making fun, which was good because that was the last thing he needed right now.

Instead, Ryder's voice read to him as fond—not amused, but warm.

The term he was searching for was warm.

He felt that way quite a bit about Ryder, that there was a genuine warmth to the man that he didn't quite understand.

Not yet.

And he certainly wasn't going to learn anything in his condition.

"Are you suggesting that I drink more often?" He raised an eyebrow, or tried to, and grinned at Ryder. "Or that I have anything to be stressed about?"

Nothing at all. He'd just lost his husband, whatever could he be stressed about?

He'd been to a party. He'd seen the evil ex. He'd seen his friends—not as part of a couple but as a single guy.

Except he hadn't been, had he?

He'd been there with Ryder on his arm, confident and sure, friendly. The man was a total package.

"No, sir. I'm saying that, every now and again, having a glass of wine or a beer makes you a better person. You've had a ton of change in your life recently. That shit's stressful, pardon my French." Ryder sounded like he knew what he was speaking of.

"I speak fluent French, you know. That is not French. But it's pardoned anyway. I'd like to be a better person so remind me of this talk when I'm sober." He leaned back and closed his eyes. It was a lot and he was tired. So damn tired.

"You don't worry about it, Mister Charlie. You're all right. I got your back." A soft chuckle wrapped around him. "You mind if I put on some music?"

He waved one hand. He didn't care so long as it wasn't awful, and he could always turn it off.

He knew how.

The soft, gentle country song started playing, low and easy, Ryder just singing along.

"Mm. That's nice. You have a good voice. I bet you like karaoke. Don't ask me to sing. I'm terrible."

"I have sung before, yes, sir. Roper and I sang a lot in different bars. We were even in choir in high school." That drawl was deepening, smoothing out.

Charles thought it was a bit like being wrapped in a warm, puffy comforter—not too heavy, not too hot. Just perfectly held.

"What's it like, having a twin?" It was an odd question for his hour and probably too personal, but he wanted to hear Ryder talk some more.

"I don't know. I mean, I've never not had a twin. This is the longest that I've ever spent without seeing him. I don't know how to even explain how weird this is. We've literally been together most every day for damn near thirty years. It's like having your best friend with you forever—since the beginning. We literally share DNA." It almost sounded like Ryder was tearing up. "Until I moved here, I could count on two hands the number of times I'd slept in a room by myself."

"Oh my goodness, I had no idea you were working through all of that. I'm so sorry. You must miss him terribly. Please let me know when you plan to see him next. I will have my travel agent take care of you." That was the least he could do for Ryder considering how good Ryder had been to him.

"He's on the road, but if he comes close to us, I'll ask for time off." An icy cold bottle of water was pressed into his hand. "The top's off. Be careful."

"Thank you." He took a long drink, letting the cold water ground him as it landed in his stomach. "Oh. That's nice." He turned to Ryder, admiring the way the crisp shirt stretched just a little across the cowboy's chest. "You know, I told Brady I didn't think I needed company. I was so wrong."

"You seemed like you were damn lonely. Folks aren't meant to be all alone."

"Alone and lonely aren't always the same thing." He'd thought a lot about that while Tad was in a coma. "I've been lonely for a long time, just not alone. I could handle the one by itself, but both is tougher than I expected."

He'd had way too much to drink, and he needed to stop talking. He took another sip of his water and looked out the window, but all he could see were streaks of light as they drove uptown.

"Well, sure. That makes a ton of sense, and you don't have to. I'm here to help, and I think we're getting on pretty good."

He turned back to Ryder and smiled. "We are. You're special. I hope you know that about yourself."

"Oh, that's awful kind of you to say. I wish... I'd sure like it to be true."

Charles nodded. He'd felt a similar way about himself at one time. "I don't have any reason to lie."

"Me either. You're not going to remember this talk tomorrow anyway."

"I might." He winked at Ryder as the car stopped outside his building. Ryder had a point though. Maybe that would be for the best since he shouldn't be saying all of this anyway. "Or I might not. But you will."

"Yes, sir. Let's get you upstairs and comfy. That suit can't be comfortable." Ryder eased him up and out of the car, hands warm and gentle on him.

"I'm ready to get rid of the tie. I don't really like ties, but one has to wear them with a suit, right? On the other hand, it's a nice suit." He just went along, feeling heavy and tired, letting Ryder steer him. He trusted Ryder to get him home.

Ryder hummed and helped, moving him through the building and up to his apartment. "Do you want to head straight for your bedroom, or do you want to visit a bit in the front room?"

If he sat down right now he would just fall asleep. "Oh, no. No. I should go to bed. I'm tired. I'll just go to my room." He shrugged out of his suit jacket feeling warm now that he was inside.

"Fair enough. Let me help you get settled. I'll grab you water, vitamin B, and Tylenol. It'll help for the morning."

"Okay. I'm going to—I'll see you." He was drunk. Definitely drunk and he needed to get out of Ryder's hair.

"I'll be right there, sir. I got you, okay? No stress."

What a kind, service-oriented man.

"No stress," he echoed, making his way back to his bedroom. He pulled off his tie and tossed it over his butler stand. He got as far as opening his belt before he flopped onto his bed, feet hanging over the side.

Oh. Spinning. That wasn't good.

"Oh, Mister Charlie..." Warm hands removed his shoes and socks, then helped him sit up. "I have some vitamins and water for you, now."

"Water." He nodded. He just wanted to go to sleep, and those hands were so warm and strong.

"Yep. Take these, and I'll get you settled in the bed, okay?"

He was given the pills, a bottle of water, then Ryder started working his shirt off.

He popped the little pills in his mouth, then switched the bottle to his other hand to drink so Ryder could help him with his shirt. A little voice was whispering to him that this was wildly inappropriate, but he decided Ryder was stronger than that whisper and ignored it. Ryder's hands were steady and gentle, and he was enjoying the touch.

The *help*. He was enjoying the help. Not the touch, that really was wildly inappropriate.

Even if it was true.

Soon he was tucked in his bed, that soft voice singing to him, easing him.

"I didn't think to ask for a companion that could sing lullabies, so I got lucky." He took Ryder's hand and held it as his eyes closed. "Thank you."

"You're welcome, sir. Get some good rest. I'll see you in the morning." Ryder didn't leave him, though.

That warm hand stayed in his until he fell asleep.

8

———————

Ryder made oatmeal and toast for breakfast because he didn't know what Mister Charlie would want. He let the man sleep in, just sitting in one of the big windows, coffee in hand.

Lord have mercy, that had been one weird-assed night, but he thought he'd done okay. He'd called Roper, who'd said he was solid, that everything was good on his end too.

No one would have found him in this big old place a year ago, but a year ago he was a different man on a different path. Now he had a salary and benefits and paid vacation and shit, and he was working for—maybe even serving some—an older man with not just a big place, but with a big life to go with it.

He guessed the whole thing was going to work for him, at least for a while. It really was an easy life, and he had all the books available on earth, so he was solid.

He was going to have to watch himself, remind himself every day that Mister Charlie was not his friend, not someone who cared about him, any more than a decent person cared about anyone.

He was the help.

"Good morning." Charles was dressed in soft pants and a loose shirt with the sleeves rolled up. "I'm following the scent of hot coffee."

"There's a pot, sir. Have a seat." He stood up, taking his book with him to stow in the bedroom once he'd poured out. "How's the head?"

"Mm. I have a very undignified hangover, but it could be worse. Do I have anything on my calendar today?" Charles sat in a comfy chair and rested an ankle on one knee.

"No, sir." He peeked at his phone, just to be sure. Nope. Excellent. Go him. It didn't take much to fix Charles's coffee, heat up his own, and deliver the cup. "Let me go put this away, and I'll get your breakfast together when you're ready."

Charles took the coffee and blew on it. "Go easy on breakfast, I'm not sure how my stomach is going to handle food."

"I made oatmeal, and there's toast. You just let me know." Poor, sweet man.

"Oatmeal sounds nice. With a little cinnamon maybe." Charles's eyes were on him, watching him.

"You got it." It was keeping warm in the slow cooker deal. Thank God for Google. "You want cream in your oatmeal?"

He was going to do banana, maple syrup, and pecans. Assuming there were pecans.

Did New York apartments come with pecans?

When Charles wasn't watching him from the living room, he was cradling his mug in both hands and sipping it reverently. "Oh, this hits the spot."

"Good deal." He delivered the bowl of oatmeal, pondering those pecans. "You need more, sir?"

"Not yet, thank you. Have you eaten? Would you care to join me?" Charles gestured to the chair across from his.

"I haven't. Give me a couple minutes to make my bowl. Do you know if there are pecans here, by any chance?"

"Here in the apartment, I very much doubt it. I haven't stocked much in the kitchen since I usually eat out so much when I'm here. I imagine you can find some down the street at the market."

"Ah. No worries. I don't need them." He made his banana-maple oatmeal, adding some granola for crunch. "Do you want toast?"

"No, thank you. I think I'll just see how this sits first." Charles looked better already though, he had more color in his face and his eyes looked brighter.

"The pills should have helped. I had a little sorority gal tell me about them, years ago." And she'd been no bigger than a minute.

"I only vaguely remember you giving something to me. I was—I apologize, Ryder. That was very poor and irresponsible behavior on my part. I'm rather embarrassed, to be completely honest. I recall asking questions and—other things I shouldn't have asked of that were very much outside your scope of employment with me."

"I didn't take advantage, I swear." But he got what Charles meant. It was just reiterating what he'd told himself this morning.

He wasn't a friend. He wasn't supposed to be sharing.

"Oh, no. I didn't mean that. I only meant that it was probably awkward for you; you didn't sign on to do all of that. But it was much appreciated."

He didn't know what the appropriate thing to say was. He didn't know how to do this, or how to feel, or whether or not he was supposed to feel anything. Likely not. "You were fine. You did fine."

Charles nodded. "Well, in any case, you're a very special person, Ryder. Thank you." Charles took another sip of his coffee.

"Thank you, sir." What did he do now? What did he talk about? What did he say? "Everyone I spoke with was real nice."

"They're a good group for the most part. Victor and I have known each other a long time, so it felt as if it would be a good place to start. There are always a few bad eggs and, unfortunately, Lewis is one of them and turns up nearly everywhere. I doubt that will be the last time we run into him. I'd completely forgotten him, to be honest, but I'll be better prepared the next time."

"He was an ass. No redeeming qualities last night." He had to wink. Had to.

"Zero," Charles agreed. "Just so. I knew you were a keeper." After a few more bites of his oatmeal, Charles seemed to be more relaxed. "I think I'd like soup for lunch. Chicken noodle or perhaps minestrone. And a nice crusty bread. You should be able to buy all of that close by. I suspect there will be an afternoon nap in my future as well."

He grabbed his phone and started a list. He'd buy himself some pecans and a fancy coffee and something to mail to Roper, plus the twins, Momma, and Daddy. "Yes, sir. What are you wanting for supper?"

"Keep it light. Maybe Caesar salad? I love a good Caesar dressing and some tasty croutons. A little chicken on it is nice too. And maybe a glass of wine." Charles winked at him. "I do remember some of our conversation."

He chuckled softly but nodded. "Yes, sir." He texted himself a note.

He'd buy his booze on his dime.

"I find it difficult to believe you've only been with me for a week or so. Don't you? It seems so easy. I thought it would take some getting used to, having a stranger in my house. But you don't feel like a stranger."

Well, that was a blessing. "I'm so glad. I'm learning a lot, but I'm tickled I'm not making you miserable."

"On the contrary. I think we're getting along quite well." Charles's sharp blue eyes flashed with fun. "It even appears to me that you've forgiven my poor judgment last night, which has made me feel very far from miserable indeed."

"Oh, let me tell you, I have been accused of poor judgment more than once." Mister Charlie had no idea. "You weren't close."

"Oh my. That sounds like the sort of story you should tell me if I'm ever that drunk again. Which I don't intend to be. You might be safe."

"Well, one way or the other, I'll make sure you're safe, coming and going." He could manage that, all the way.

Charles had been looking at him so strangely all morning. Studying him like he was looking for something. "I'd like some more coffee, please."

"Yes, sir. You done oatmealing too?" He stood and picked up his dishes.

Charles handed off his bowl, then pulled out his phone and started scrolling. "I am done. Thank you, it was delicious. Did you make it yourself?"

Did it come froze? Could you order it in? Because he'd

eaten the shit from the packet. Lots. This was way better. "Yes, sir."

"I'm so impressed with your cooking, I really am. When I'm here, I usually buy some bagels and call breakfast handled. The oatmeal was very nice."

"I'm tickled you like it. I'm feeling my way around lots of this, so there's bound to be a few disasters. So far? I've lucked out." And he was grateful for it.

Of course, he'd never even heard of minestroney, so he'd be testing that…

"Don't worry, I'll be sure to let you know." Charles shook his head and looked back at his phone.

"Yes, sir." He finished his oatmeal in a couple of quick bites while he made them both another cup of coffee, delivering Mister Charlie's before doing the dishes.

He was going to have to Google Map a grocery store, a liquor store, and a place to buy soup…

9

———

Charles picked up his phone to call Ryder's placement service as soon as Ryder walked out the door to go shopping. He'd been drunk last night no question, but not so inebriated that he couldn't recall most of the evening.

He remembered his conversation with River well enough. Vividly, in fact. River had assumed he and Ryder were lovers, and not only that, River had extended an invitation to Charles to bring Ryder to his men's club. He was aware that River and Victor were members, and it wasn't the first time he'd been invited. Tad hadn't ever cared to go, so they'd turned down an invitation more than once.

He wasn't sure he completely understood the goings-on there, but River and Victor were both upstanding, good to their partners and otherwise friendly and kind. If he and Ryder were more than they were to each other, he felt as if he'd consider accepting.

But he and Ryder—

It had been a long time since anyone was as attentive and gentle with him as Ryder, and his feelings about it were confusing. He was paying the man to work and to be that very thing for him, but Ryder had gone above and beyond last night. And not just last night—to be fair, Ryder was much too good at his job.

He sighed and shook his head at himself. Hungover or not, he couldn't indulge in this kind of navel-gazing. Ryder had a job to do and he did it well. Period.

Period.

He dialed Rog, his contact at the placement service.

"Good morning, this is Rog. How can I be of service?" The man's voice was smooth as silk.

"Hello, Rog. This is Charles Martin. Everything is fine, I wondered though if you might have a moment to talk."

"Mr. Martin!" There was a moment of pure shock. "Of course. Is everything going well with Ryder?"

"Very well. Remarkably well. He's really a lovely person, a wonderful chef, and he has an extraordinary mind for details." Even details he wouldn't have thought about for himself.

"I'm tickled to hear that. He's new to the company."

"He's a good find, and you did well sending him to me." He'd just fess up and get Rog off the phone. "I wanted to make you aware that I probably pushed the boundaries of his contract last night before you heard it from him. Embarrassingly, I had much too much to drink, and he was very kind in getting me home and in bed. If you have a bonus system, I'd very much like to make sure he's recognized. Anything I can do to contribute, please let me know."

"Mr. Martin, believe me. Ryder isn't going to call and complain over a small indiscretion. For a rodeo cowboy, he's amazingly patient." There was the oddest tone in Rog's voice.

"Well, I felt it was important that I tell you, just to

validate anything he might mention. He is patient; you're right. To say the least. He takes excellent care of me, far beyond anything I might have expected. It's hard to believe this is his first position."

"Well, I'm glad he's pleasing. He seems perfectly suited, and I haven't heard a single peep from him since he started."

"Hopefully that's good news." He felt like there was something he should be asking, like whether there was anything he should know that wasn't in Ryder's dossier, but he supposed if it wasn't there, it really wasn't his business. "I don't want to take up too much of your time, I just wanted to be—honest about everything."

"Of course. Absolutely. Please let me know if you need anything. Anything at all."

"Thank you. I will do that. Have a good day." He hung up but couldn't help thinking there was more to Ryder than he understood. He tapped his chin with his phone, wondering if he should just let it go, but curiosity was still getting the better of him.

He finally gave in and googled Ryder, shocked to find thousands of responses. There were pictures of two little black-haired cowboys, side-by-side, in matching jeans and boots. Silver-haired teenagers—one in long braids, one in a crew cut—in their high school graduation robes. Then there were all the bull riding photos, silver buckles, bruises—always the twins.

Then there was a photo of four young men—Ryder and his twin along with two younger boys, obviously twins as well.

The last photos were of Ryder in the hospital, tubes coming out of Ryder, head shaved, and his twin was right there, holding Ryder's hand, a rope with a lock tattooed on the twin's wrist.

That was obviously the career-ending wreck Ryder told him about. Poor man, that looked painful. It was amazing though, how his twin really did look just like him. The tattoo was interesting. He figured it was some bull rider thing so he googled that next.

"Rope with lock tattoo," he said out loud as he typed it into his phone.

Unity and freedom. Protection. Submission.

He took the time to read that again but he couldn't be sure he really understood what he was looking at. Unity and freedom, fine. Protection was a little esoteric, but also fine. Submission...to what? Or whom? Was it religious? Maybe it was a cowboy thing. He didn't know the first thing about cowboys, when it came down to it. Other than he thought Ryder looked great in dressy jeans.

Also, the man who had gone into the wreck seemed at least ten years younger than the man who had come out. He couldn't say for sure, but it seemed to him that the end of one's career coupled with some kind of obvious head injury would naturally change a person. Such a shame.

Not that Ryder seemed terribly unhappy. He'd taken to the job well. He was friendly and easygoing; he seemed well-adjusted enough. Maybe he'd had some excellent therapy.

All the photos fascinated him, and then Charles found that the twins had a fan club.

A fan club.

It was still active, or at least he thought it was, but all the new information was about Roper—where he was riding, what he was doing.

That had to be tough for Ryder, being out of that loop. He talked about his brother all the time too, so he certainly had to feel like he was missing everything.

It was a shame there was so little he could do about it. It wasn't as if he was free to just follow the rodeo around.

Much.

He typed around, discovering that the bull riders would be in Connecticut in ten days.

Huh. Charles knew Ryder knew the bull riders were coming. He had to. He spoke to his brother dozens of times per day.

He wasn't sure why Ryder hadn't said anything, but perhaps the man had planned to take some days off. Driving to Connecticut was a shorter trip than to New York City, and one could argue that it was on the way, mostly, so why shouldn't he go? He'd never been to the rodeo. He'd ask Ryder to make all the arrangements.

That might be...fascinating.

In fact, it would be eye-opening. He hoped Ryder would be interested in introducing him around.

CHARLES

Come see me when you're back from your errands. Bring tea, please.

He texted Ryder, smiling to himself, then set his phone down on the end table.

RYDER

Yes, sir. What's your position on chocolate croissants?

Chocolate and croissants were two words that he never said no to.

CHARLES

I've never met one I didn't like.

RYDER

Excellent. These look amazing.

A picture showed up a second later, the pastries brown and flaky and delicious-looking.

They looked lovely. He was certain he didn't need them, but he wanted them.

CHARLES

Thank you.

RYDER

see you soon. Found minestroney

Minestroney? He laughed.

CHARLES

Minestrone. It means "soup" in Italian.

It was comfort food.

RYDER

Huh. In Spanish it's sopa. Smells good.
Bbiab

Bbiab? What did that mean? He'd never seen that one before. Tad had been up on these things, but he was clueless. Better believe I am, buddy? Best before it's all blue? *Google again.*

He googled it and it made much more sense. Be back in a bit.

CHARLES

See you then.

Tad would have typed something like "cu" but he couldn't bring himself to text in anything but full sentences.

About an hour later, when he was beginning to get worried, his phone rang, and it was Ryder.

"Uh, they—the security dude? He doesn't seem to think I belong here, and your mini-strone is getting cold."

Hadn't he walked by with Ryder half a dozen times? Had they not seen Ryder leaving the building a couple of hours ago? "Is that Leonard? May I speak with him, please?"

"Surely. Are you Leonard? Mr. Martin would like to speak to you."

"Apologies if I've made a mistake, Mr. Martin, but—"

"It's fine, Leonard. That's Mr. Vales, my personal assistant. Ryder Vales. Make a note, please? He needs to come and go freely. I'm sure if you ask, you'll find I've given him a key to my apartment."

He heard the tinkling of a key on a chain, and he could see that bland look on Ryder's face as clear as if he were down there.

"Ah. Yes, sir. I will put Mr. Uh—"

"Vales. Ryder Vales," he replied just as dryly.

"Mr. Vales. Thank you, sir."

"Thank you, Leonard. Have a wonderful day."

He really shouldn't pick on Leonard, but he wasn't sure what was really going on, and he intended for security to treat Ryder with respect.

"Good deal. I'm heading up." There was a wealth of amusement in those few words.

"See you soon," He chuckled outright, just because he could. Also, he was pleased with himself for thinking up a way to reward Ryder for his work and also learn a little more about the man at the same time.

There was a sharp knock at the door. "You close enough to let me in? I'm teetering!"

"I am! Hold on." He hopped up and hurried to the door to open it. "Tea-tering? Hm? Very clever."

"I'm a smart dog." There was tea, soup, bags from a handful of shops—was that a huge baguette? Goodness.

"Oh. Here, let me help." He took his tea and some of the packages and set them down. "It appears you had a busy morning. I apologize for Leonard."

"It's no big thing. I didn't have on my good hat, just my cap." Ryder started unpacking bags, putting out croissants, a baguette, some sort of butter and honey, a quart of soup, cheese. Then there were a couple of bags with different trinkets and T-shirts that Ryder put aside. "Here's your receipts for the soup and the rest of the food."

"Thank you." He didn't need receipts; he trusted Ryder, but the cowboy brought them dutifully every time he spent any money. He'd given up saying he didn't need them. "The soup smells good. Where did you find it?"

"This deli down the street. It smelled good and had nice bread, and the man there had a good smile." Ryder gathered up his bags. "I'll get these out of the way."

"Souvenirs?" He had to ask before Ryder whisked them all away.

"Yes, sir. For my brothers and folks, plus a couple friends. My baby brothers have never been here."

The baby brothers must be the other set of twins he saw in that picture. He couldn't ask, of course, because Ryder would know instantly that he'd been snooping on the internet. But now felt like a good time to hatch his little surprise. "Will your brother be riding in Connecticut?"

There went that head-tilt again. It was a sweet little tell. "He is. He's riding good this year. He's in the top ten."

There were a number of ways to ask his next question, and Charles quickly weighed them, setting on one that would make it clear that he wanted to go, and that it wasn't just a favor, or worse, meddling. "Would you be interested in taking me to see the rodeo?"

Tilt.

"Well, I'd love to. I was intending to go, but we can go together—" Ryder pursed his lips, eyebrows drawing together. "Not as work, though, if you don't mind. I'll get us tickets, and we'll just go as people. Fair?"

Hm. Well, now he was worried that he'd thrown a wrench into Ryder's private plans. "Oh, I hadn't intended for you to be working at all. It was just an impulsive thought on my part, and it certainly wasn't my intention to impose. We could go another time when you have more notice. I—I thought it might be fun, and I might learn a little more about you and your long career. Perhaps there's a better time for you."

"Did I say something that meant no? I said I'd love to, and that I'd like to go together as folks, and that I'd get our ticket..."

He huffed a laugh. "No, not specifically, but I suddenly realized I was imposing myself into your life, and maybe you'd prefer that I didn't."

"No. Not at all. Everyone should get to see a good bull riding. I'll make arrangements for us."

"Excellent. Please use my card for tickets and hotel rooms and whatever else we need." He sat with his tea and took a sip, letting it warm him all the way through.

"How do you want to get there? Plane? Train? Automobile?"

"Oh, my driver can take us. It's only a few hours. Just a little shorter than the ride into the city, in fact." Ryder could tell him everything he needed to know on the drive.

"I love that idea. No having to fight for parking. This event's at a casino, so it's always a challenge."

"He can pull right up. We'll look important."

"Excellent. I'll take care of everything. It should be fun." That was a pleased smile, warm.

Ryder always seemed happiest when he had a project. Something to accomplish. "I'm very much looking forward to it. I haven't done anything new to me in many years. I hope you will tell me everything I need to know."

"You'll be fine. You'll have a great narrator, trust me."

"I do trust you." He grinned. "And I like that. My narrator."

"Yes, sir. I'll explain the sport, introduce the people, and tell you which bulls are rank." Ryder grinned for him, those demon-dark eyes sparkling.

"They rank the bulls? Interesting."

"They do, the better the bull, the more rank they're considered. The best ones are in the short-go. That's the final round. The event is three days—Friday night, Saturday night, and Sunday afternoon."

"Oh wonderful. By Sunday, I might feel like I understand the sport a bit." He was genuinely excited about going, which also made him realize how disappointed he would have been if Ryder hadn't wanted him to come along.

"I'll help. I want you to meet my brother, too. He's a hoot."

"I am always happy to meet family. I think this is going to be quite the event." And so far out of his comfort zone it might as well be Mars, but Charles felt as if it was going to be good for him to do something different. Something he and Tad would never have done.

"It's a good one. Not as good as a Dallas or a Houston— the bulls don't have near as far to travel to those, but good nonetheless." Ryder kept talking as he puttered around, doing odds and ends that made the apartment more comfortable—straightening a pillow, closing a curtain, opening a window.

He sipped his tea and watched. All of this seemed rather out of character for the bull riders in his head—tough as nails, covered in dirt—looking at this man he'd never guess what his former profession was. "Would you care to share one of those croissants you bought?"

"I bought them to share, of course. I got a ham one too, because I was curious as all get out. Like the ham and cheese is baked in, not a sandwich. Hot or not?"

"Ham and cheese should be hot. Chocolate should be warm." He was an expert on pastries; they were his favorite indulgence.

Although that key lime pie that Ryder had snuck into this study? That might be a very close second.

"Do you want both or just the sweet?" Ryder grinned at him. "They're as big as your head."

"Oh, just the sweet for me, and only half. I don't need a whole one." He knew that bakery. They made sweets big enough to feed three people.

"Then we'll share. I just couldn't resist that scent." The whistling disappeared into the kitchen.

Such a sweet boy.

Man. Young man?

Boy just seemed to fit Ryder for some reason. Not that he would ever say such a thing out loud. Goodness. How condescending would that be? Ryder wasn't twelve.

He was much too lovely in an adult way to be twelve.

What is in this tea? Rein it in, Charles.

It didn't take long at all before the croissant, halved, two plates, two forks, and napkins appeared.

"Mm. Smell that? Have a seat and eat with me. I have a meeting later, yes? And do I have dinner plans? After dinner plans?" He hardly looked at his calendar anymore; he just waited for Ryder to tell him what was happening next. Fairly soon he thought he might even start referring people to Ryder to get on his calendar.

"You have a meeting at two, and you needed to call a Mr. Arwen before, you asked for Caesar salad with croutons and chicken and wine for supper, and you are free as a bird this evening."

"Oh. Excellent. Let's take a walk later if it's not too chilly." He loved to walk when he was here, especially at night. He loved the lights and people watching, the occasional musician on the corner.

"No problem. That sounds like fun. I like exploring." Ryder waited for him to take a bite.

So polite.

He cut a piece off with the side of his fork and held it up like one would for a toast, then put the fork in his mouth, knowing before he bit down that it was going to be amazing.

It was even better than he'd expected.

"Oh. Mmm. Mhm." He nodded approval as the not-too-sweet chocolate melted on his tongue.

"Good?"

"Uhn."

"Yay!" Ryder took a bite, and his eyes crossed in obvious bliss.

"See?" He took another bite and this time the flakey pastry hit his tongue first, so buttery and lush.

"Okay, this is amazing. I think that I have to learn how to do this..."

"You know, everyone else I know would say something like 'I can't wait to go back to that place', but not you. You just said, 'I have to learn how to do this.' You're unique, Ryder. Different. Creative. I appreciate those things about you."

Ryder beamed at him. "Well, I have to go back, see if they'll tell me how. If they won't, I'll look it up. Google and Amazon and YouTube are my friends."

"Good luck. There is a lot of competition in this city. They actually might not tell you."

Ryder shrugged. "That's okay. Can't hurt to ask. The worst they can say is no."

"I don't know about that. This is New York. They could say many worse things. Many. With a lot of cursing." He laughed and took another bite.

Ryder wrinkled his nose. "I'll have to channel Roper then. He can snap back like nothing going."

"He's a brave one, hm? He sounds like someone who doesn't mind getting himself in trouble." And very different than Ryder that way.

"He loves trouble. Loves it." Ryder chuckled, the sound low and soft, fond.

"And that's why you say you had to take care of him?" He wondered who did that for Roper now that Ryder wasn't there.

"He's totally grown-up. He's just less...picky. I like to be in a nice space, if that makes sense."

"It does." He understood what Ryder meant, even without meeting Roper. "I prefer to be in a nice space as well."

"Yes. I can tell. I am trying to keep it done right for you."

"You're doing an excellent job." The acknowledgement and praise always seemed to make Ryder happy. "I'm very pleased."

He preferred for Ryder to be happy.

"Good deal. This would be awkward if you disliked me."

"If I did, you wouldn't be here." He winked at Ryder and sipped his tea. "The truth is, I don't know how I managed before you arrived. You've been good to me."

"Thank you. I'm trying. This is my first time."

"I know. It's difficult to believe given how good you are at it." He glanced at his watch to make sure he wasn't going to miss his phone call.

"Do you want your soup at noon? One?" Ryder licked a bit of chocolate off his fingers.

He watched for a second but while it was good to feel like he wasn't dead yet, it was also completely inappropriate.

"Well, a two o'clock meeting, a phone call before…let's say twelve-thirty."

Ryder nodded and set an alarm on his phone. "Twelve-thirty it is. Baguette or are you carbed out 'til supper?"

"Just the soup will be enough after that midmorning snack. I think." He didn't have the metabolism he used to.

"Yeah. I hear you. I got enough of the soup to try. There's nothing in it I don't like."

"You'll like it. It's Italian comfort food. And it has so much flavor."

"Beans. Pasta. Veggies. All good." Ryder started cleaning up their snack. "You holler if you need me. I'll be here."

"I will do that. Thank you, Ryder. Let me know if you need anything from me for our reservations in Connecticut." Ryder had his miles card, so there probably wasn't much else he needed but it seemed polite to offer.

"Yes, sir. I'm on it." He got a warm, happy little smile. "I'm excited."

He could tell. That bright smile said it all. "Me too." He was very much looking forward to it, to learning about the rodeo and to spending some off-the-clock time with Ryder.

10

"Roper? Roper, you're supposed to be at a signing in five minutes, boy. I will beat your ass."

They were waiting to check into the hotel, and Ryder glanced up, meeting Cord's eyes.

"Wrong twin."

"No. No, you are not doing this to me again! He's retired. He's not here. You are always—"

Ryder winked at Mister Charlie and shook his head as Cord ranted and railed.

Poor man. Roper had broken him a decade ago.

"Excuse me. Hello?" Charles stuck out a hand. "Hi. I'm Charles Martin, and I can promise you this is the retired twin."

Cord stood there for a second, eyes huge, neck going deep red, veins sticking out. "I hate twins. Hate them. You tell your brothers they are not allowed on tour!"

Charles pulled his hand back, looking a little taken aback. "Well, it's uh...been a pleasure."

"Cord! You be nice. Mister Charlie here has paid for his

ticket, and so have I. Don't you be rude." He wouldn't stand for that nonsense. Cord was raised better.

Cord blinked again, turned a deep purple, then nodded and held out his hand. "You're right. I'm sorry. Cord Gruene. Pleased to meet you. I hope you have an amazing night."

Charles shook, still looking a little unsure of Cord and glanced at him before speaking. "Thanks. I do too. I'll keep this twin out of your hair, I promise."

"I'll hold you to that. One is enough. Sorry, Ry."

"No worries. I'll make sure Roper's at the signing booth." It had been his job for years, after all.

"So when you're not working for me, you're working for him?" Charles's tone was teasing. "And... Mister Charlie, hm?"

"What?" Had he said that out loud? Seriously? "I just check on him. He gets into trouble."

"I imagine he's been surviving without you for a while."

"You'd think so." He found a smile, but part of him was a little worried. "I'm not talking to him on your time, I swear. I'm just a brother."

Charles put a warm hand on his arm. "Ryder, you can talk to him any time you please. There is no 'on my time' when it comes to family."

He took a deep breath, then reached out and patted Charles's arm. "Thank you. I appreciate that."

He didn't know how to say no when Roper asked.

Charles gave him a nod. "Okay. So, who was that guy? Really?"

"He's the sponsor liaison. He has a terrible job. He has to make the sponsors happy and make cowboys show up on time." It was a pointless job.

"Oh? And is he actually able to fulfill either purpose?" Charles seemed to be catching on quickly.

"Nope. Not a chance. He's always yelling or getting yelled at." No fun at all.

"No wonder he was in such a poor humor. I hope he is well compensated for his efforts."

"I guess?" He didn't know. He didn't really care what all the guys in all the moving parts made. No one ever bitched, so it had to be good.

"So what's first after we check in? The initial round is tonight?"

"I got us a suite, so we can go on to the room, get cleaned up, and then we can go see all the vendors, have a snack, whatever you want." He wanted to go say hi to folks, introduce Charles around. "The event starts at seven, and we have family seats."

"Family seats sound very nice. I want to see everything, so I am letting you lead the way."

They finally made it up to the desk and got checked in. Charles signed all the paperwork and didn't blink at the cost of the suite.

The bellman took their bags, and they wandered toward the elevator banks.

"Ryder? Ryder, is that you?" Mackey, the head bullfighter waved at him. The man was magical. He could always tell them apart.

"Mackey!" He waved back, and Charles turned to follow as he went to say hello.

"That no good brother of yours didn't tell me you'd be here. Does he know?" Mackey looked at Charles and held out a hand. "Mackey. Pleased."

"Charles. Likewise." Charles shook with him.

"He knows. He's... Roper."

"He's a shit, but we all love him. You're looking so much better than last time we saw you. Y'all heading up?"

"Yes, sir."

"Me too. I left my knee pads upstairs." Mackey chuckled and shook his head.

Charles held the elevator door for the bellman and everyone else. "Interesting. Are knee pads standard gear for bull riders?"

"I'm a bullfighter. Cowboy protection. I work for a living, right, Ry?"

"You know it." Ryder owed Mackey and the other bullfighters his life. "Mackey is the head bullfighter. He keeps us safe."

"That sounds like quite a responsibility. You'll have to forgive my ignorance; this is, in fact, my first rodeo." Charles was proud of that little joke he could tell, and it was adorable.

"Oh, wow. Good deal! Well, Ry here knows every inch of the show. He won't steer you wrong." Mackey chuckled softly. "You got yourself the good one, for sure. Roper is... wild and wooly."

Oh God...

Charles looked amused. "Have I? Good to know."

The elevator opened on their floor, saving him from whatever Mackey might have said next.

"See you tonight, Mackey."

"Yessir. Y'all have fun." Mackey waved, and they headed down to their suite.

"I got myself the good one?" Charles was grinning as he opened the suite door.

"Well..." Shit. "Roper is not really suited to this sort of thing..."

At all.

"Good twin, bad twin? I've heard of such things. I'm even more curious to meet him. Oh. The suite is quite nice."

Charles let the bellman bring the suitcases into the room, then slipped him a tip. "Thank you."

"Thanks. He'll run up and meet you in a bit, if that's okay." He was nervous for Charles to meet Roper, a little bit.

Roper was far more interesting than he was.

"He doesn't need to go out of his way. I'm sure he's busy."

"He's staying two floors down. I let him know to text when he was done signing posters."

"All right then. We can get settled in the meantime." Charles looked around. "Which room is mine?"

"The bigger one. It's got a Jacuzzi tub, and it's supposed to have the good view." And Mister Charlie deserved those.

"Oh, very nice." Charles dragged his suitcase into the bedroom. "Yes, very nice, indeed. Am I dressed appropriately? Should I change?"

Did Mister Charlie even own jeans?

"This is casual—jeans and a button-down, or a T-shirt. Be comfortable. I can iron for you, if you need it."

Charles popped his head out of the bedroom. "Casual merits an iron?"

He shrugged. "I iron my jeans to crease them."

His shirts were pre-starched at the cleaners.

"I had noticed that when we went to the party at Victor's, but I thought that was considered dressy. Interesting." Charles disappeared again. "I think mine are fine. No one would ever mistake me for a cowboy anyway."

"Rodeo fans come from all over the world. Don't worry on it. You'll be perfect."

"I know I'll have fun, in any case. I feel like a VIP sitting in the family section with a retired rider, watching people you know. I've been eagerly anticipating this weekend since we talked about it." Charles had been talking from behind a partially closed door. When he came back out, he was wearing jeans, black boots with a thick sole, and a black button-down shirt. "Does this work?"

Oh, wasn't that a pretty sight. "Yes, sir. You're right as rain. Let me go switch shirts right quick, so we can be ready for whatever."

Every so often, Charles made him swallow hard.

His phone vibrated with a text from Roper as he was getting changed.

ROPER

I'm about to knock!

And, with basically no warning, there was a loud knock on the door.

"Is that Roper? I'll get it."

"Okay." He hurried to unbutton his shirt, hearing Roper's voice ring out.

"You're Mister Charlie! Pleased. You're cute as all get out. How's it going? Have you put Ryder over your knee yet?"

"Have I—well. Goodness. You must be Roper. I prefer Charles, if you don't mind."

Oh, for fuck's sake.

RYDER

Don't get me fired, man. I like this job

He heard Roper's phone ding, then, "Oh, sure. Of course. Sorry. Sorry, I'm just playing. Ry has said tons of great things about you. I'm glad you came out. This is a solid event."

Oh, better.

He got his shirt on and buttoned, then he started tucking in.

"Well, I certainly am looking forward to it. Come in, please. Would you like something to drink? I believe you'll find soda and water in the mini-fridge. Ryder is just changing after our trip."

Roper didn't drink before he rode. It made him puke.

"Oh, that's kind, but I never drink before I ride, thanks."

He opened the door, and there was his twin. God, it had been weeks.

"Ry. Damn. You look amazing." Roper hugged him tight. "Missed you."

"Yeah." He couldn't hardly talk.

He was surprised how well Charles read the room. "You know, we need some ice. I saw a machine down the hall. I'll be right back." Charles picked up the ice bucket and the door closed softly behind him.

"He's cute."

"Still. Nice."

"Sorry. Headaches?"

"Not as bad. Your shoulder?"

"Hurts."

"Doc?"

"Nah."

Their conversation flew fast and furious, both of them knowing the answers to things before the other asked the questions.

"Standings are good."

"I'm riding good." Roper sighed. "Still doesn't feel right with you not here."

"I hear you." But he couldn't just follow Roper around and not ride.

His wreck had damn near killed him. He wouldn't survive another one. Hell, he was still supposed to be wearing a helmet, or so the Doc said.

His brain was solid, and his skull was...okay.

"Yeah." Roper nodded, hearing his thoughts. "But you

got a good thing going now. Seriously, has he spanked you yet?" Roper grinned wide, changing the subject as only he could.

"Shut up. He isn't—he's a new widower." Ryder was pretty sure that Charles wasn't into sex, and if he was, he was going for someone classy. "I'm the *help*, Bubba."

"That's not creepy."

"It's what it is. It's okay. I like him."

Roper gave him a bit of the hairy eyeball but let it go.

"Found the ice." Charles came back in and set the bucket down on top of the mini-fridge. "The two of you really do look alike. I'm pretty sure I wouldn't get you confused like that gentleman we met earlier though."

"No? That would be a trick. Mackey's the only one who doesn't. Right, Ry?"

He nodded. "Even Momma can't tell."

"Oh, I don't believe that for a second. But you can test me at some point and see how it goes." Charles winked at him and sat. "So, Roper, I hear you're having a good season."

"That's what they tell me. I'm solid to make the finals, and I'm healthy. At this point, that's the secret. We're getting closer to our finals event every day."

"That's great. When are finals?"

"October. I'm excited as all get out." Roper glanced at him. "You'll be there, right, Ry?"

"If you make it, I'll be there, Bubba." It was only right.

Charles nodded. "I'll make sure of it, Roper. Not to worry. You just stay healthy, as you say, and he'll be there."

They both stared at Charles, and Ryder wanted to just howl at Roper and say, "See? A good man."

"Thank you, sir," they said, in unison.

"You're welcome, boys." Charles chuckled and got up off the couch. "You have an event to get to Roper, so don't let us keep you. Ryder is going to walk me around a little. Maybe get a bite to eat."

"Oh, the boozy milkshakes are amazing!"

He arched an eyebrow at Roper. "You're eating milkshakes?"

"Stole a suck." Roper winked at him.

"Hm. I could be convinced to try one of those."

"That sounds amazing. Let's do it." Ryder hugged Roper again. "Good ride tonight."

"I'll show off, just for you."

Charles was quiet but stepped in a little closer, a strong presence behind his shoulder. "I'd be happy to buy a round of drinks after if you're interested. Just let Ryder know if you feel up to it."

"Sounds perfect. I'll see y'all in a few hours. Love you, Ry."

"Love you more."

Some things were eternal.

Charles held the door for Roper, then let it close quietly behind him, smiling slowly. "He's very handsome."

Ryder chuckled, because he got it. Roper had something special. A spark. "He knows it too."

Charles rolled his eyes. "And you don't?"

"Oh, I totally do. He's something else. Tons of personality." He made sure he was looking good. "You want to go wander?"

"You do realize you're his twin, don't you? I was talking about you, Ryder. You look exactly alike."

"Now you said you could tell us apart..." He had to tease.

"Oh ho! Touche. Well, you pointed out the difference between you already. He knows, you don't." Charles opened the door for him. "Shall we?"

"I'd love to. Let's go play." He was so ready.

11

———

Charles had never seen so many cowboy hats in one place. If he hadn't known this was Connecticut, he'd have sworn he was in Texas. Ryder led him through a vendor fair at the venue with tables and tents that had everything from riding gear to hats to music to food that looked and smelled amazing.

They'd had tacos, which he'd managed to eat without spilling all over himself, and now he was looking at the menu for the adult milkshakes Roper had been talking about.

"Jack Daniels and caramel? I believe we have a winner."

"Ooh... I want the one with Irish cream and malted milk balls. That sounds like heaven." Ryder's dark eyes simply shone.

"All right." Charles stepped up and ordered himself the salted caramel with Jack, and the Irish cream concoction for Ryder. They were much bigger than he had anticipated and he laughed as he handed a shake to Ryder. "Do people usually finish these?"

"God, I hope not. That's twice the size of me, altogether!" Ryder grinned wide, and his expression was young, eager. "I do love whipped cream, though."

"As do I." He took the straw in his teeth and took a sip, startled for a moment by the sweet, the sharp bite of the whiskey, the cold ice cream, and the warmth from the booze that followed. "Oh, my."

Ryder glanced up at him, tongue sliding through the whipped cream and chocolate. "Good?"

He hadn't had enough to drink yet to use the alcohol as an excuse for staring, but he couldn't help himself. Worse, he was fairly certain Ryder had noticed. "Delicious." That came out a little thick, so he cleared his throat and tried again. "Extraordinary."

"I'm glad. You want to try mine? I'll share."

"Why not? You can try mine too." He bent to Ryder's offered straw and took a sip in as non-suggestive a manner as he could muster. The Irish cream was smoother than his Jack Daniels and the shake tasted more like candy than whiskey. "Ooh. Very smooth."

He pushed his over, and Ryder leaned close to take a sip.

"Ooh...that's yummy." Ryder licked his lips.

"A little more of a bite, right? But the caramel, mmm." And he was feeling it a little already. Must be all the sugar. That tended to make the buzz stronger. "I saw you admiring the stone in that bolo. What was it? Moonstone? It was lovely."

"I think so, yes. It's our birthstone, you know? It's neater than diamond or the pink one."

"Is it? That's very nice. I thought it was a very handsome piece. April babies, hm?"

"Yessir. The twenty-second. Four, two, two."

"And your twin brothers? When were they born?" He took another sip of his milkshake, and it made him shiver. "Ooh. Strong."

"Christmas Eve." Ryder drank deep as well.

"That's interesting. I always wondered what that was like—being born on Christmas or New Year's Day or Leap Year." He wasn't sure he'd like that, but then again, it was something different. Something that made you interesting to other people.

"When's your birthday?" Ryder actually sounded interested.

"January 17. I'm a winter boy. Capricorn. Very on the cusp of Aquarius." He used to know a lot about astrology, but he hadn't thought about it in years. Had to be the whiskey.

"Oh, I get that. I'm on the day of—between Taurus and Aries. Our dad is a Taurus, our mom is a Capricorn, so..." Ryder chuckled softly. "Honestly, I have no idea what that means."

He laughed. "Well, Taurus is stable and stubborn, Aries is spontaneous and loves adventure. So, essentially, you got the Taurus and Roper the Aries." His mother, like him, was hardworking, practical and somewhat pessimistic. Recently he'd begun to understand what they said about Capricorns aging backward, and he liked it.

"Roper was first, so I can believe it." Ryder pulled a malted milk ball out of the milkshake and popped it in his mouth.

"My mother was an Aries too. Beautiful. Always coming and going. She had a large group of friends and boyfriends." She hadn't been the most present mother, but she'd been a good person, a happy person. Kind.

"Wow. Our mom is a school teacher now; dad is a cowboy. They were both rodeo people once."

"Where do your parents live?"

"Silver City, New Mexico. They love it there."

"Did they ever travel to see you both ride?"

"Oh, absolutely. When it's closer to home—Midwest, Southwest, West Coast. They're right there." Ryder smiled, the expression warm, fond. "They're exceptional parents."

"They sound it. How old are your twin brothers?" He was curious, and they were here as just people, as Ryder had said, so he didn't feel like questions were out of bounds.

"They'll be eighteen this year. Crazy boys."

Eighteen. So young. "Are they riding too?"

"They're junior bronc riders, and they like to rope, too. Lasso and Latigo saw us beat ourselves half to death."

"Given your names, I get the impression this was going to be a rodeo family one way or the other," he said dryly.

"My mom still races sometimes, and Daddy ropes, so yes. We're not super famous, just an old rodeo family." Ryder tilted his head. "What about you? Do you have a lot of family?"

"No. I had my mom, but she passed away right before I met Tad. And my father, well, I told you about him. I do remember my mother's parents a little." His mother raised him modestly, but she'd come from money. "I would have liked to have siblings, but my mother was happy with just me I guess."

"I'm real sorry for your losses, sir." Ryder almost reached out for his hand. "You've had so many."

"Seems like it, doesn't it?" He shrugged. "I think that's one of the reasons I wasn't sure I wanted to hire anyone after I—after Tad died. But I do appreciate your company." He took Ryder's hand and held it for a second, then slowly let it go and pushed his drink away. "Hm. I think I've had plenty of that."

"You made a dent in it, yessir." Ryder's smile was warm, focused on him. This was dangerous.

He needed to put a little space between them.

He took a breath and stood up slowly in case he was more tipsy than he realized, but he was fine. Buzzed, no question, but steady. "Care to walk a bit more? Do you think we should find our seats soon?"

"Let's wander. There are a few of my former sponsors I'd like to show my face to."

"Lead the way." He followed Ryder back out into the crowd. They hadn't gotten very far when a big man in a black hat bumped into Ryder, knocking him back a step. He caught Ryder instinctively by the shoulders to keep him upright.

"Sorry, man. Whoa! Hang on. Roper? Ryder? Which one are you?"

"Ryder. How's it going, Hank?" Ryder didn't sound incredibly pleased to see this Hank.

"Fair, fair." Hank was looking Charles over as he spoke. "I see you've kept yourself busy since you hit your head."

Ryder moved to where he was between him and Hank, protecting him. "Yep. Busy and happy. You doing well?"

Ryder, who was half this man's size, was getting between them. Anyone else might think that laughable, but he knew Ryder was tough. He'd seen the YouTube videos.

"Fine, Fine. No need to get defensive, boy."

"I'm Charles." He'd just be friendly. He wasn't afraid, but he wasn't keen on the idea of Ryder getting in a fight. And why did it seem like every big man they came across was aggressive around Ryder, anyway?

"Pleased. I'm Hank." The big man shook his hand, and

he narrowly avoided making it a competition. "It's good to see you on your feet again, Ryder."

"Thank you. I'm tickled as all get out that I got out with all my brain cells." Ryder offered him a tight smile. "Have a great event."

That was a clear "go away", if he'd ever heard one.

"I plan to. Enjoy watching." Hank looked him up and down again before nodding to Ryder and walking away.

"You've got your hackles up," he said softly as Hank stepped back into the crowd. "He was looking at me as if I might be competition." He'd been off the market for a long while, but he understood jealousy when he saw it.

"He and I used to be close. We're not now." Ryder's voice was tight, bordering on angry.

It was difficult to resist the urge to give Ryder a warm hug. Another part of him wanted to follow Hank and give the man a taste of his knuckles. "I understand it's none of my business, but all the same, I am very sure that it's his loss."

"I'm a little bit your business, but thanks. I did the saying no, and I was right to do so, but it made things harsh—folks talk."

Charles sighed. "He aired your private business. I'm sorry."

"Yes. He did. He sucks. You, on the other hand, are a decent human being. Thank God."

That made him smile. "Thank you. I do try. And for what it's worth, I don't mind letting people think I'm your private business now." He winked at Ryder.

Ryder chuckled softly, cheeks gone pink. "Well, I think folks are making assumptions, and I don't mind."

They were definitely making assumptions. There had

been certain moments today when parts of him wanted to make assumptions too.

He didn't plan to assume anything. What people said about assumptions was typically correct.

And he wasn't going to think that way.

He couldn't.

Even if he found himself wanting to.

"Who's the guy standing on the fence?"

"That's the gate, and he's pulling Pistol's rope." This was surprisingly fun, telling Mister Charlie everything the man didn't know about bull riding.

They had amazing seats—three rows up, in between Rope Canutt's family and Skylar Paulson's. Apparently they were having a vacation together.

"Like pulling it tight, you mean?" Charles was glued to the chutes, watching everything and so curious. Charles leaned closer. "No wonder those bulls seem so annoyed."

"It's not annoyance. It's genetic. Seriously, it's bred into them. If they were uncomfortable, they wouldn't buck."

"Oh, no. I was kidding." Charles touched his knee for a very brief second. "I did some reading before this trip about how athletic these bulls are. Now, me? I'd be annoyed."

"I—Yeah." Folks didn't do that. Not even gay ones. He knew there were some handcuffs and ankle...cuffs? But tight around the middle?

Nope.

The gate opened and Charles watched intently. He was just as disappointed as everyone else when the ride only lasted five seconds. "Bummer. That was quite a landing though. These guys can really take a beating."

"Yes, sir." It was a brutal sport, and getting hurt was inevitable. It was just a matter of how bad and when.

"Oh! That's...uh. Mack? Right?" Charles pointed to the bullfighter. "He just gets right in that bull's way. Wow."

"Yes. He's the team lead, and he's fearless. He's together with the sound guy. His best friend is the safety man. The guy on the horse. He's a bit of an asshole, but he's okay." And a horndog and a half.

Times three.

Charles chuckled. "An okay asshole. Well, I love watching him ride, as if he and that horse have one mind or something."

"I've never met anyone better, and my brothers and folks are all riders." It wasn't that he didn't know how, of course he did. He'd just been riding bulls for a long damn time.

Charles nodded and watched the next several bulls out of the chute with interest. He asked about scoring and how they picked the bulls. He asked about the order of the riders. He asked what the payout was everyone was gunning for. "So some riders have helmets and some have hats...?"

"The helmets are safer, but some riders feel like they mess with your balance. Some riders just want the hat. It's a preference thing. Some leagues made it necessary, but ours hasn't." He hadn't worn one, but he was a balance rider, not a strength one. Roper didn't wear one either.

"How well is Roper really riding? He said he thinks he'll make the finals. Do you think he could win? Is he *that* good?"

What was he supposed to say? No? He didn't think so? He thought Roper would make some good money and have a good time but not win. "The numbers aren't in his favor to win the whole thing, but he can win tonight's event, or any number of things."

Charles nodded. "He's your family, so that wasn't a fair question, I suppose. I am looking forward to watching him ride regardless." Charles bumped shoulders with him in a friendly, supportive way.

"He's good. Damn good. Better than me." Now, at any rate. He'd been damn fine, once upon a time.

"Better than you? Are you sure?" Charles leaned back in his seat. "I have a confession to make. I googled you."

"Of course you did." That made perfect sense. "I googled you too. We're living together. It would be silly to not make sure we weren't serial killers, right?"

Charles snorted. "I suppose I'm naive. I hadn't thought to google you until I found out you'd been a bull rider. I trusted the agency to send me someone without serial killer tendencies. Then again, I fully expected to decide within days that I didn't need or want an assistant."

"Well, I've never worked for an agency. I wouldn't have, if it hadn't been for Roper, you know? I never would have thought of it." And wouldn't that have been a shame?

"Roper got you the job? Did he know someone?"

"Yes, sir. He and the owner had been, uh, boyfriends." His cheeks were going to set on fire.

"Ah. Well, it's good to have connections. I'm glad this one worked out in your favor, if not theirs."

"Oh, they're still friends. They were just bad together, I guess. Roper said Rog wasn't into the same stuff." And that was enough information, full stop.

It didn't seem like Charles thought anything of it. "And as you can see, I didn't fire you, so it's working out well for us. I'm having a good time and we still have the whole weekend—whoa! That guy made it! That was amazing!"

They all cheered, and he watched the score come up. Oh, a ninety. The confetti guns were—

BANG!

They were suddenly covered in colored paper.

"Oh!" Charles jumped and then started to laugh and waved his arms in the falling confetti. "You didn't warn me!"

"Ninety-point rides get confetti!" He cracked up, taking a single piece to save for his collection. He'd date it later.

"Thanks." Charles was grinning and his eyes lit up in a way that made him look so much younger than he was. He noticed that Charles took two pieces for himself, which then disappeared into the man's pockets. "We need more ninety-pointers. That was amazing."

"Who's the newbie, Ryder?" Rope's husband leaned over to grin at him.

Oh Lord. "This is my good friend, Mr." *Charlie.* "Charles."

That was almost a whoops.

"Hey, Charles. I'm Jude. Welcome to the family section."

"Thank you very much. I feel so privileged."

"Are you enjoying the show?"

"I really am. This is so much fun. I'm just amazed by these riders."

Jude nodded approvingly. "There will be more confetti. And some other fun things."

"Looking forward to it." Charles was surprisingly friendly for someone who had seemed so introverted at first.

"Where are the babies, y'all?" Between them, Sky and Beckett and Rope and Jude had five ranging in age from two to twelve.

Sky chuckled. "Staying with Beck's folks at our place."

Jude nodded. "Ours are with Rope's parents. This is a short but grown-up vacation."

Charles still seemed giddy from the confetti. "Speaking

of grown-up, have you tried the adult milkshakes? You really must try them."

"Ooh..." Sky and Beck spoke together, while Rope and Jude gave each other a meaningful glance.

"We have to get some after the event."

"Highly recommended. Roper's suggestion." Charles was watching the riders again.

Beckett's eyes rolled. "Should have known. I bet he's glad to have you here, Ryder."

"He's doing fine without me."

Sky caught his gaze, winked. He got it. Sky hadn't quit on his own terms either.

"Both of those things can be true at the same time." Charles stretched out an arm and rested it along the back of his seat.

"I think you're right." He offered Charles a smile, unsure if he should lean back into the touch or not. He decided to relax. If Charles moved, that would let him know.

"When does he ride?" Charles asked—without moving. "How do they decide what order?"

"There are five sections. The top ten will ride in the short-go. The top three riders tonight will be in the money. And then they do it all over again tomorrow." He let himself just breathe and relax.

"So we get to watch the same guys have another shot tomorrow?" Charles's arm was still resting on his seat—not his shoulders, but he could feel the man's warmth all the same.

"And Saturday. Then the Sunday short-go is for the event win and the big money. The points are cumulative."

"Got it. Do people put money on this sport like they do on football and such?"

"I'm sure they do, but—I mean, there are a ton of

variables, right?" The bull, injuries, the cowboy, whether they threw the ride—it would be way more chance than he was willing to risk money on.

Charles shrugged. "I would guess so. I'm not a betting man. I was just curious." The next ride was very good. Not a ninety-plus, but respectable. Charles moved his arm long enough to applaud the cowboy, and when that arm came back Charles gave his shoulder a squeeze. "That was great. My heart is in my throat every time these cowboys dismount though."

"Oh, I hear that. I have seen some wrecks."

He'd survived some wrecks. He'd barely survived the last wreck.

"I'm sure." It was gratifying that Charles was interested. He had a lot of questions, and they seemed to be out of genuine curiosity. "Is there a halftime? A time to get a bite and something to drink? Or do we just come and go?"

"You mostly come and go. There will be a ten-fifteen-minute break between the main go and the short-go, but that's toward the end." He offered Charles a smile. "If you need anything, I'll be happy to hook you up."

"Oh, I was just thinking something cold to drink would be nice. You're not on the clock. I can get it for myself."

"I know." He did, but he didn't mind. He liked knowing Mister Charlie was settled. "Do you want water, Coke, a beer?"

"A Coke would be very nice, thank you." Charles pulled out his wallet.

"My treat. You bought the milkshakes." He winked at Charles and stood. "Y'all need anything from concessions?" He didn't think so. He didn't think the guys were even watching the show, really.

They all shook their heads as he passed. "Nope. We're good. Thanks, man."

He felt Charles's eyes on him as he headed through the stands.

Ryder got stopped at least a half dozen times on the way through to stand in line, but it wasn't terrible.

Folks had been concerned, were glad to see him and, all in all, it felt good.

He stood, flipping through texts when one of Hank's buddies came to stand next to him. "Hey, man."

"Back of the line is there." He wasn't being paid to be polite anymore.

"Thanks. You're looking good. Is retirement treating you well?"

"Yessir. I'm having a good time. Staying busy." And he didn't want to say anything that could get misunderstood.

Not at all.

"Listen, I know it was weird after the thing with Hank and all, but I was really sorry about your accident, and I'm glad to see you up on your feet again."

"Thanks." Okay, he could be polite. He knew how. "I was laid low for a bit, but I'm up and moving. I appreciate all the donations."

"This business can be generous sometimes. Anyway, it was good to see you." The guy—whose name Ryder just couldn't recall at the moment—tipped his hat and headed for the back of the line.

"Ryder? Roper. No, you have to be Ryder, Roper's gonna ride soon. Can I get a picture?"

"Of course." He smiled without a single thought, macking for the camera. He had done this ten-thousand times, easy.

The woman smiled with him, put her arm around his

waist, and her friend took a bunch of pictures. "Thank you so much. So cool to see you here. Wish your brother a good ride." She took a step back, and he was suddenly next in line.

"Hey, there. Can I please get a Coke, a Diet Coke, and two waters?" His head tilted. "Can I have some of the fries with the cheese and all too?"

"Yep. One disco fries!" the cashier called out and rang him up while a young lady filled their drinks and grabbed a cardboard basket of fries from under a warmer. "Enjoy the show."

"Yes, ma'am. Thank you." He was damn lucky he knew how to carry shit, and even luckier when a teenager with peach fuzz on his cheeks offered to walk him down to his seat.

He let him, passed the food down to Mister Charlie, then signed the kid's league cap for him. "Thank you. I appreciate it."

"Thank you, sir." It got even better for the kid when Rope and Sky signed the cap as well. The kid left with a big smile on his face.

"My refreshments have been delivered by a celebrity," Charles winked at him as he took his seat. "I'd forgotten that you'd have fans here. How wonderful. I'm quite lucky."

He didn't know quite what to say to that, so he grinned and handed over the French fries. "I got us a snack."

"These look evil. Look at all that cheese." Charles held it on one knee where he could reach easily and took a sip of his Coke. "Your friends are kind. They kept me entertained while you were gone with stories about how they'd met. Skyler said he was champion before he was forced to retire."

"He was. He was one of the best. He taught us all a ton, honest to God."

"I don't doubt it. He seems to really care about you and other younger riders. He says he's even coached your brother a couple of times."

"Yessir." He raised his voice. "Not that he could tell us apart."

Sky's voice floated back to him, tone dry. "Your own momma can't tell you apart."

"She says she don't have to. She made us interchangeable." He winked at Mister Charlie.

Charles chuckled and helped himself to another cheesy French fry.

"Yes, she's right. You're both a couple of dumbasses."

Rope laughed outright at that one, and Charles snorted.

"You think? You're just pissed that you aged out, cowboy." He winked at Charles, because he hadn't even done that.

"Older and wiser, kid. Older and wiser." He could hear the amusement in Sky's voice.

Charles nodded sagely, grinning. He was obviously enjoying the banter. "Indeed."

"Older, that's for sure. Wiser? I guess y'all got that grampa thing going on..."

"Hey!" He wasn't sure which one hollered, but someone did.

"Now, y'all. Let's not start a fistfight in the family section."

That was followed by a lot of laughter, all the way down the row.

"Roper's up next." He nodded toward his brother, who was having Buck Daniels pull his rope these days. He was sad, and for a minute he wanted to be over there helping.

"Oh. I can't wait." Charles set the fries down and put a

hand on his knee, giving it a light squeeze as if he knew how Ryder was feeling.

Roper searched for him, and he lifted his chin, waiting for their eyes to meet. When they did, he whispered, "Good ride, Bubba."

Roper grinned wide, then gave him the thumbs up.

Okay. Okay, it was going to be okay.

"Look at that smile." Charles's hand was still resting on his knee, warm and solid, grounding him.

"Yep. He's ready." He never yelled when Roper rode. He watched, and he willed his brother to stick.

The gate opened, and Mister Charlie leaned forward, not yelling either, but watching intently. He could tell Mister Charlie was sending good energy Roper's way.

One. Come on. Come on.

The bull was going into Roper's hand, which was good for him, and the son of a bitch was spurring to beat the band.

Two. Don't you slide.

Three. Correct! Come on, Bubba.

Four. Five.

"Hang on, you son of a bitch!" Sky hollered. "Don't you dare let go!"

Six.

Roper was going down in the well, the bull spinning like a damn washing machine, those heels snapping toward the lights.

Seven.

Eight.

He stood up, bellaring at the top of his lungs. "Yes! Get off! Get off, Bubba! You did it!"

Charles stood with him, whispering, "Careful, Roper."

Roper's hand was caught in the bull rope, and for a wild

minute, he thought his twin wasn't going to be able to get out. He was already moving, climbing over the empty seats in front of them, when Roper's hand popped out and he went flying.

"No." Charles reached out and grabbed his shirt, pulling him back. "Not your job."

"I—" His heart was slamming against his rib cage, rattling his bones.

"Mackey will keep him safe. Breathe, Ryder." Charles kept a hand on him, steadying him on his feet.

Roper found his feet, then headed for them and climbed the fence. "Did you see, Ry?"

He knew that meant, *I'm okay. Don't worry. I was scared, but I'm okay.*

"I did. Good ride!" He settled back into his chair with Charles, a cold sweat covering him.

"Good ride, Roper." Charles gave Roper a quick round of applause and sat as well. That arm settled behind him again, but this time on his shoulders, not the chair. "What do you need?"

He blinked a little. Nobody ever actually asked him that. "I guess—I'm... I'm good?"

He wasn't sure because his hands were shaking just a little bit as he had his Coke, but it settled out pretty quick.

"You are okay, and Roper is safe, but is this too much? Do you need a break?" Charles's thumb was stroking his shoulder.

He did, but he wasn't sure that he could, not with Rope and Sky and them just sitting up there watching. He thought that maybe Sky would get it.

But Rope? Rope was one of those lucky sons of bitches who'd just managed to not ever get too-too bad hurt.

"Let's take a walk." Charles stood and offered him a hand up.

"Sounds good. Let's go." He took the hand without thinking about it too terrible hard. Then he let Mister Charlie lead him up and out of the stands.

Mister Charlie just nodded to Sky and Rope and everyone as they went by like this was just normal, like they were going to get a beer or whatever, and nobody seemed to think anything of it. But they didn't stop at concessions, they walked right on by and ended up in a quieter spot away from all of the noise.

"I hope you don't mind that I just made the decision for you. You seem a bit shaken, and I thought you could use a quiet minute."

"I might could use it, for sure. It's the first time I've been back." It was the first time he'd been to an event since he retired. The first time without his skull in thirty pieces. The first time he was able to attend without barfing.

But he wasn't going to say that. He was just gonna stick with—this was his first time back.

"I wondered if that was the case. You seem to be having a bit of a trauma reaction." Charles rubbed his back, warm palm moving in slow circles.

"I'm sorry. That's embarrassing. I apologize." His cheeks were on fire. He thought he'd been ready. He had to be ready.

"Not in the least. It just means you're human." Mister Charlie's voice was low and soothing. "It's a perfectly natural reaction to be worried about your brother now that you fully understand what a wreck means."

"Yeah. I don't remember it, though. Not at all. I remember getting on the plane at the airport on the way to the event, then being in the hospital."

"It's possible that part of you does remember it. But emotionally, you understand it all the same. You're not here to take care of your brother anymore. Now, all you can do is support him."

His belly drew in, and he suddenly felt a cold chill flood him. "I think I need some water."

Charles's hands were on him, moving him to a bench. "Sit. Close your eyes. I'll get you a bottle." He was alone suddenly, as Charles hurried off.

Oh, God.

Oh, God.

He was such an idiot. What was he doing? What the hell was wrong with him? Mister Charlie was getting *him* water!

"A sip. Slowly." It felt like Mister Charlie had been gone forever but was back, sat beside him now and holding the bottle for him.

He took a small sip, and he could hear it splash in his belly. "I'm so sorry. Please forgive me." *Please don't tell on me.*

"I don't understand. Forgive you for what? You don't have anything to apologize for. Have another sip." Mister Charlie held the bottle to his lips again.

He took another drink, a deep breath. His cheeks were burning, but he managed to talk himself down out of this weird-assed tree he'd climbed.

"How is your head?" Mister Charlie touched it like he was checking for a fever, then looked into his eyes. "I think we should go back to the hotel. There will be more riding tomorrow."

"I think... I think that's a good idea. I'll text Roper. He'll have to do after parties and stuff." And he was embarrassed and ashamed, and he needed a shower.

He felt dirty, as if he'd done something bad.

Mister Charlie helped him up. "Tell him he's welcome to come to the suite to see you any time."

"I will. Are you sure? You'll miss the winner. I don't want to ruin your first event." Ryder cared about Charles.

He got a smile and Charles touched his chin. "There are other nights. I saw Roper ride. That was enough for the first night. You need a little quiet time, and I want to look after you, as you always look after me. Come on."

"Okay...yes, sir." He had to force himself not to dip his head into the touch.

"Good boy." Mister Charlie smiled at him as they made their way out of the venue.

12

―――――

Charles escorted Ryder back to their suite and sat him on the couch in the common room while he found another bottle of water. Making sure the cowboy got some rest was easy enough, but something else was bothering him.

That apology.

Why on earth would Ryder feel like he needed to apologize so profusely—even to the extent of asking for forgiveness—for something like this? Something that was perfectly understandable, human, and over which Ryder obviously had no control in any case?

It bothered him. Upset him even. He didn't understand.

Ryder was pale as milk, cheeks sporting a flush almost like a fever.

"Are you still feeling sick? Would you prefer to go lie down?" He sat with Ryder, close enough that the man might take some comfort in his presence. He couldn't imagine what Ryder was going through, what horrors he'd seen when, for a moment, Roper couldn't seem to get free of the bull. He felt compelled to help, though, any manner Ryder would let him.

"No. No, I'm solid. I just got a shot of adrenaline, that's all." Ryder found him a smile that was almost not-shaky.

"You don't have to smile, Ryder. You don't have to be okay. If you are, wonderful, but if not, you can be honest. You can tell me. We're friends, right?" At least friends. He wasn't going to lie to himself either. Ryder was starting to feel closer.

"We are. I feel stupid for freaking out. I'm not the type to, you know?"

"Nor am I, but it's happened on occasion. Are you the keep it all in and carry on type? I know that trap well. You have to let yourself feel what you're feeling; it's the only way to move beyond it."

"That's tough for cowboys. We're taught not to. You know, cowboy up or get in the truck and all that. I just... I'm always the one who's close enough to get him, but I don't like being scared."

"I feel like your reaction was bigger than being scared. Has he never had a close call before? Surely this is not the first time. It's just your first time back."

"Exactly. We're bull riders. We have close calls all the time. This is the first one since the big wreck." Ryder shook his head. "It was serious enough that Doc said I couldn't come back."

"That had to be a terrible moment."

"I knew before anyone said." Ryder was calming down as they sat together. "My folks came out, all my brothers. My grampa and gran. All of them. They thought it was over."

Ryder's family had to have been terrified. "But it wasn't, and you're here. Recovery takes strength; moving on to something new takes courage."

"You know it. I had no idea what to do. Roper was the one who suggested I try this. He says I'm made for it."

He couldn't disagree. "And what do you think?"

"I like taking care of things to make your life better. It's... incredibly satisfying."

He had to smile. "I find it quite satisfying myself." He hadn't ever thought of himself as the type of man who would benefit from someone like Ryder. At this point, Ryder was so much more than a personal assistant. It wasn't just a job for Ryder, and he didn't feel like an employer.

Ryder touched his hand. "I'm sorry you lost your husband, but I hope I make things a little better, easier."

"Thank you. We've both lost something important to us, haven't we?" He rested a hand on Ryder's thigh. "Better and easier, both. You are a gift I didn't know I needed."

Ryder's cheeks went bright pink, and he could see that his words were affecting the cowboy, causing a bulge in his jeans.

He slid his hand away slowly. Ryder had had an emotional day, and Charles wasn't sure he had a handle on his own at the moment. "The way you've taken this on—it's more than just a job to you, isn't it?"

"I—I thought this weekend wasn't about work." Ryder's eyes were shocked, wide and worried.

He'd hit a nerve, struck something deeper than he'd intended. "I wasn't really asking about work, was I? I'm asking about something more personal."

"Please, don't fire me. I want to...be this for you. It's important." Ryder's throat worked as he swallowed convulsively.

Please don't... "What?" He leaned a little so he could look into Ryder's eyes. "What? Ryder. Fire you? Whatever for?" Had he sounded upset? Had he given Ryder that impression? How could he possibly? He couldn't imagine life without Ryder right now.

Ryder took his hand, holding on. "I know you're mourning. I know I'm not supposed to feel things for you, but—I swear I'm going to be good to you."

Oh God. What could he possibly say to that? That Ryder was already good to him? That the cowboy's dark eyes and sweet smile had him thinking in a way he wasn't sure he should? Or maybe that he'd mourned Tad long, long ago and losing him was sad, but inevitable. Or maybe—

Maybe he'd skip the words altogether.

Charles took Ryder by the chin and kissed him with more force than he'd intended, but very much on par with everything he was feeling.

Ryder opened up with a gasp, holding back for only a breath before leaning right into his kiss, those near-black eyes holding his gaze.

He broke the kiss suddenly and pulled back enough to properly return the look. He finally understood what he wanted to say. "I will be good to you too."

"I think I'd like that, very much." Then Ryder gave him a sweet, long, almost gentle kiss.

He accepted it, smiling to himself and relaxing. He thought he understood the plea for forgiveness now, and he hoped Ryder understood that. He also knew they had a great deal of discussion ahead of them. But this moment didn't need discussion; this moment only needed consent.

Ryder cupped his jaw, thumb rubbing his cheek, the touch unbearably soft.

He sank back into the couch and pulled Ryder closer, letting himself indulge, fingers roaming over Ryder's torso.

They breathed together, nice and slow, and he could feel

the steady beating of Ryder's heart, the pulse thrumming against him.

He tugged on Ryder's shirt to untuck it and, while Ryder worked on the buttons, he loosened the belt around that tight waist. He wanted to see, to watch those hard abs move under his fingers.

Ryder shivered for him, the tiniest little moan escaping the man. It surprised him, sounding so loud in the silence of the room.

He sucked in a breath at the sudden ache in his balls as his body seemed to wake up for the first time in a long, long while. He helped Ryder remove the shirt, then tugged open those starched Wranglers, eyes glued to the tight, muscled body.

There was a smattering of scars, some that looked surgical, but more seemed random. One crescent-shaped scar had a tiny bucking bull inked on it.

He touched and investigated, allowing himself to simmer in the heat between them, enjoying the buzz of his arousal. "Beautiful," he said, but the word may have been lost in a low growl.

"You have amazing hands." Ryder's legs moved restlessly, caught in his jeans.

"You have an incredible body." He touched the tattoo, dragging a finger over it. "Clever."

Ryder's entire body rippled. "Yeah. It was the first hoof mark. I had to celebrate it."

"The first." He shook his head, smiling slightly. He couldn't pretend to understand what went on in Ryder's head, but it was certainly genetic. "Most of us would have decided once was enough."

"I was raised with it, and once Roper tossed in his hat, I

was right there." Ryder stretched up tall, the bull seeming to buck.

He slid his hands up Ryder's sides. "Undress for me. I want to see the rest of you." Narrow hips, strong thighs, a pretty cock.

Ryder blinked, rolling away to pull off his boots and socks, then he stood, easing his jeans off. That left that fine body in nothing but a clinging pair of forest green boxer briefs.

He gave Ryder a smile, admiring him with great appreciation as his own cock filled his jeans. "Thank you." He stood, stepping close and looped an arm around Ryder's back. "You're gorgeous. You don't mind being admired, do you?"

Ryder's cheeks went bright red. "Admired? It feels real nice, to know you like what you see."

He bent to kiss Ryder again, have another taste of the man who wanted nothing more than to be good to him. "Darling Ryder, I'd have to be a fool not to."

He stroked one tiny nipple to hardness, and Ryder pushed up on tiptoe, demanding more. More touch. More kisses. More of him.

There was plenty of him, and Ryder was welcome to it. He loved that Ryder never asked for anything for himself but was demanding now. He held the man off a little because he enjoyed the build-up, and he also liked the little grunt of protest he got from Ryder as he pulled his hands away to unbutton his own shirt.

Ryder's cock was heavy, thick, leaving a wet spot on the boxer briefs, fingers tangling with his as he tried to help.

"Patience," he said softly, but he withdrew his hands and let Ryder finish with his shirt. "There's no rush."

"That's something new."

He imagined so. He didn't think long and slow was in Ryder's repertoire.

He shrugged his shirt off. He wasn't ripped like Ryder, or as young either, but he wasn't ashamed of his physique or the hair on his chest—some of which was tinged with white.

"I think you might like it, even if it's new."

"I think you're right." The trail of glory disappearing under Ryder's waistband was black as pitch, a stark contrast to the silver hair on his head.

He traced that line and tucked one finger under the elastic, giving it a light snap before cupping his whole hand over the bulge under the fabric.

Ryder's prick swelled and jerked under his hand, and his eyes crossed.

"So needy." Charles could have been talking about either of them as his own cock answered in kind. He rubbed firmly, measuring up Ryder's graceful cock and hefty balls.

"Gonna make me embarrass myself."

Charles could get used to that throaty, desperate tone of voice. "No. Never be embarrassed. It feels good to be wanted. I hadn't expected anyone to feel that way about me again." That was a deep and private truth. He knew he would find company if he wanted it, but he never thought anyone would see him—look at him the way Ryder was looking at him—ever again.

"Oh, honey. You're hot as hell." Ryder stepped into his space, face lifted for another kiss.

He heard that, but there was more in Ryder's eyes than heat. He could see it.

For a man who was used to being in a hurry, Ryder's kisses were remarkably sweet. He savored it, tongue exploring, tangling with Ryder's, tasting curiously.

Ryder's hands were rough, callused, and they made his skin sing, his eyes rolling back in his head.

He grunted, the sound rumbling in his chest as he opened his jeans to give his cock more room, then took a step forward, backing Ryder past the couch and toward his bedroom in the suite. He didn't object to making love on a couch—or anywhere really—but not for a first time, and especially not *this* first time. He wanted to be comfortable. He wanted Ryder to feel safe and cared for.

Not only that, but he needed to assure himself that Ryder understood how special this was.

He bent to remove his boots once they reached the bedroom and set them aside, then straightened up to slip out of his jeans. "Unfortunately, I'm not...prepared. I certainly didn't have this in mind when we left the lake house."

"No. I didn't either, but we can make each other feel good in a bunch of different ways." Ryder stroked his belly, petting him.

"No doubt." He kicked his jeans aside and let Ryder get a look at him in his black boxer briefs. "You've proven yourself to be resourceful."

"I am a smart dog. Trust me." Ryder winked up at him, licking his lips and wetting them.

That was an invitation he was looking forward to accepting. He kissed those lips again and lifted Ryder to set him on the bed. Ryder was smaller, but all muscle, and more solid than he'd expected.

"Mmm...strong." Ryder rubbed their noses together, then nipped his bottom lip.

"You too." He reached for Ryder's waistband and worked those green boxers down and off, then circled his fingers loosely around Ryder's pretty cock.

Ryder spread, his lips parting on a soft little gasp. "Oh fuck…"

He took his time, learning the feel of Ryder's hot skin, the length of the thick veins, and the weight of Ryder's prick in his hand, feeling as if he'd never held another man's cock before.

It had been that long.

"Beautiful. So lovely."

"I—You have the warmest hands…" Ryder's eyes rolled back in his head, and he felt the throbbing of Ryder's cock, the flesh turgid and needy.

"Because I'm burning up over you, darling boy." He slid out of his boxer briefs and climbed over Ryder, making sure their hips lined up and their cocks slid against each other. He couldn't help his groan, it felt so good. Charles wanted Ryder every way he could have him.

Ryder's hand wrapped around his hip, helping him move, dragging their bodies harder together.

He took another kiss, stealing Ryder's breath as he rolled his hips, fascinated by this side of Ryder—so much need from a man who never asked for anything.

Ryder's abs were hard as hell, the ridges on the flat belly fascinating as they bumped the tip of his prick.

He sucked at a little bud of a nipple and pinched it between his teeth enough to make it sting a little, testing, learning what Ryder was into. Ryder gasped, body stiffening, a wild little cry splitting the air.

Oh, that was lovely.

So lovely, in fact, he tried it again on Ryder's other side, and this time the sound was softer, but Ryder couldn't keep still. Charles braced a hand on one hip and held it down. "Easy, cowboy."

And then he did it again.

One of Ryder's hands found his head, tangling in his hair. "Fuck!"

He'd never heard his cowboy curse, not really. Ryder seemed so incredibly gentle…

So far Ryder had been feisty in bed, and to be honest, that combination worked for him. He could be a bit spicy sometimes, and he thought Ryder might just be up for it.

"Such a mouth on you," he teased. "You like that, hm?" He wanted to hold the cowboy down, give him something to fight so he could feel all that strength working against him. He wanted more of those wild sounds. Mostly, he wanted inside Ryder. "I wish I'd come prepared for this."

Ryder huffed out a sharp breath, shivering the slightest bit under him. "Me too. I—I didn't even begin to think that this could be a thing."

"Not in my wildest dreams." Well, perhaps in his *wildest* dreams, but he didn't plan to admit to that. He wasn't exactly sure what this thing between them amounted to yet. Ryder wasn't just anyone; there was something more at play and he was just beginning to get his head around it.

Right now he wanted out of his head though.

"We can improvise." He caught Ryder's gaze. He reached for the hand that was still in his hair curled his fingers around Ryder's wrist, then got hold of the other wrist as well.

Ryder blinked at him, the expression sweet, hungry, and confused all at once, totally endearing. "I'm good at improvising, I think."

"I'd imagine so, with only eight seconds to get it right." He winked and kissed each wrist before moving them above Ryder's head and holding them there as he rocked firmly, pressing their hips together.

"I—I can't love on you like this..." Ryder grunted out the words even as he met Charles's strength.

"I know." And he'd graciously take no for an answer if he got one, or even anything like it, but Ryder's cock pressed right up against his hip, and he didn't think he'd hear much of that.

Ryder arched underneath him, those muscles lifting him, cock leaving wet kisses on his skin. That read very much like a yes to him.

Enough yes to make his eye cross. "Want you." Desperately, in fact. He returned the effort, and they rocked together, hips grinding, meeting each other right in the middle of give and take.

Ryder rolled his eyes, feeding Charles a moan that fed his soul. That was pure need, hot and fierce and all for him.

He took another kiss, stealing more of Ryder's breath, releasing those delicious lips just enough to say, "So close. Come on, cowboy. Don't make me wait another second. I want to feel your heat on my skin."

"Oh, fuck me. You're pure fire." The words came seconds before Ryder did.

He watched the confusion of pleasure and need cross Ryder's face, and that surrender was so sweet. "You're so lovely." He let go of Ryder's wrists so he could brace himself for a couple of final, wild thrusts and gasped as he shot, groaning through the release that his body had been begging for.

"So pretty." Ryder stroked his hair as he murmured the words, gentle little compliments that helped ease him down.

"Mmm." Charles kissed Ryder again, slow and deep, before settling along the cowboy's side. "You have a little bit of a naughty streak, darling boy."

"Mmm...only the littlest bit. Most of me is good as gold."

He nodded, wanting to pull Ryder in and protect him, though from what he wasn't sure. "You've been good to me, no question. Do you snuggle? I'd like to hold you."

Ryder blinked hard, eyelashes flashing quick. "I hate sleeping alone, so yes, sir. I sure do."

They needed to clean up, but he'd hold Ryder for a while, make sure his cowboy knew that what happening here was more than just the sex to him. "Come on, then." He rolled away a little, giving Ryder room to snuggle in.

Ryder hummed and curled right into him, sighing softly against his throat. Oh, so sweet. The cowboy was a champion snuggler.

He tucked his arms around Ryder's shoulders and hugged him close until he felt Ryder's breathing even out, then he relaxed a bit just keeping his cowboy close.

Ryder melted, quiet and solid against him.

Was this really happening?

He let Ryder rest while he took it all in. Charles let his eyes close, but his mind was busy. They were consenting adults, and he didn't mind what others thought, but this was more than sex. It was complicated and layered, and there would be so much to talk about when they woke up.

13

Ryder woke up with his entire body suffused with heat, and he sighed, humming softly.

What a lovely dream.

He'd been making love with Mister Charlie, and he'd felt sensual and sexual, aroused and arousing.

It had been magical.

Or maybe he wasn't awake after all. There was a soft sigh beside him and, as he turned to look, he felt the arm tucked over his waist.

It was warm, perfect somehow, and he'd be damned if he did anything to wake Mister Charlie. Not now.

Not with everything so warm and right for a second.

"Good morning," Mister Charlie whispered without moving a muscle, the words just as warm and gentle as he felt.

"Mornin'. You sleep good?" Because he'd slept like a fucking dream.

"I don't think I've slept as well in quite some time." Charles leaned closer and kissed his forehead. "I am very comfortable."

"I'm glad." He searched Charles's eyes. "I thought it was a dream, for a minute."

Charles's gaze was steady in return. "It certainly felt like one, didn't it?"

"Yes, sir." A good one too. His balls were still happy.

Charles sat up on one elbow, looking right into his eyes. "We're just people, remember."

Okay, what did that mean?

Were they supposed to be...aliens? Monsters? Supreme beings?

"Yes, sir."

Charles smiled gently. "What I mean is that you're not working right now, *so*..." That last word had a strange emphasis, like he was supposed to know what came next.

"I don't usually—No, I've never once woke up with someone I worked for before. I won't make you sorry, though."

"I'm not sorry. I'm happy. This is good. I believe we've made the right decision. I just want to know what you calling me 'sir' means. Right now. In bed. Since you're not working." Charles was still smiling at him and tugged at a lock of his hair. "I need to know who you are, Ryder."

"I—" Oh. Oh, God. He didn't even think about that sort of thing anymore. At all.

No matter what.

"I promise I'm not—" Bad.

"I don't care what you're not." Charles cupped his cheek, the smile turning into something warm but more serious. "I want to know what you need. I'm afraid I don't have experience in this area."

"I don't know what to say." He took a deep breath, telling himself that he'd done nothing to be ashamed of. "I'm not into things like Roper is. I tried, and I'm not that. I just want to make sure you're well taken care of."

"Ah, yes. I remember what you told me, Roper likes trouble." Charles spoke slowly and his tone was gentle. Curious and also caring. "I like the way you take care of me. I never thought of myself as a man who needed taking care of, but—" Charles's look turned thoughtful, his focus distant. "I like how you make me feel."

"I like how I make you feel, as well. It's necessary." And Ryder meant it. It felt amazing, to make things right.

"Necessary. I see." Those eyes snapped right back to his. "And you want me? You want this—with me?"

"Yes, sir." No question. He was happy with Mister Charlie, and he wanted this position in Charles's life.

That earned him a kiss. It was slow and heavy, and when Charles pulled away his look was serious. "We have a problem, Ryder."

"Okay. I'll fix it. Just tell me."

"This is something I suppose you can fix, if you're willing." Charles shifted and sighed. He seemed to be taking a second to think. "I can't pay you and also have you in my bed. So, you're going to have to let me take care of you too."

"I—Can you do that? I mean, obviously you can, like with money, but I mean, are you okay to do that?" He had a little savings, and if Charles decided to break up with him, he hadn't had a job when he'd gotten his last one...

"Aren't you kind?" Charles kissed him again, just quickly. "I am fine, thank you. I think I can figure this out. Other than disengaging with your employer and making new sleeping arrangements, I don't suppose much needs to change. And I have friends who I can, well, whom I can consult."

"I'm not trying to be a problem. I swear to you. I enjoy

being with you, being your...good and safe place." He had lots of thoughts about the things Roper did, about the things that he'd tried, and he was bad at them.

"If you were a problem, you'd be a good problem to have." Charles settled and pulled him close again, and a long, strong arm curled around his back. "I know I'm asking a lot for you to give up your income to be with me. It's important to me that you have everything you need. I don't want you to worry about your future, no matter what happens between us. I'll make you whatever deal you need up-front. I'm a fair man, I promise you."

"I guess that's something we need to chat about, sure, but I'm not—I mean, it hasn't been a job-job for a while now. Maybe since New York." What this was, was more like a calling, like a bigger thing than a man could pay for.

Charles nodded. "I know just what you mean. I just don't want to get out of bed until we're on the same page. I want to walk out of this hotel room and know where we stand."

"I don't work for you. I quit. I'm here because I want to be." That was clear, right? He'd find himself a job he could do from Charles's.

"You're the first person in my employ to ever quit, you know." Charles's chuckle rumbled in his chest, vibrating against his cheek.

"Well, I'd tell you this was the first job I ever quit, but that would be a lie." He hadn't lasted two weeks at the Dairy Queen.

"Goodness! If I'd known your track record I never would have hired you in the first place." Charles kissed his scalp and nuzzled his hair. "I think you should make up for your shortcomings by starting a nice hot shower for us."

"Mmm..." Us. He liked that idea. He liked it a lot. "Yes, sir. I'm happy to."

He'd packed the shampoo and soap that Mister Charlie liked, so he knew that the shower would be good.

"Thank you. Then I will take you out to breakfast, and we can decide what to do with our day. Did you have thoughts before the show tonight? Do you want to check in with Roper?"

"I do. I didn't have a drink with him last night, so hopefully he'll want to hang out for a minute today."

"He's welcome to join us, or I can leave you to spend some time with him on your own. Whatever you want." Charles sat them up and kissed his shoulder. "Go on. Shower, cowboy."

"Shower, shower, la la la." He winked at Charles and stretched up tall, wiggling side-to-side and loosening his spine.

"Showing off for me, are you? I'm not going to complain." Charles wasn't just looking, he was *watching*.

"I was stretching, but you can watch all you want." He winked back over his shoulder. "Hot shower, coming up."

"I like watching." Charles slid out of bed after him and stretched as well, then followed after him slowly.

He made sure the soap and shampoo were out and got the water heating. Then he grabbed down the towels, then the bath mat.

Charles leaned in the doorway and just watched. "You're graceful. Has anyone ever told you that? You move...almost like a dancer."

"Me? I mean, not really. I did ride with balance more than strength, so maybe that's it?" Ryder just tried to keep his feet.

"Maybe. Strength I can see. Balance too. Why is only the hair on your head white?" Charles reached out and pulled the shower curtain back so he could step in.

"It happened with our pappy the same way. We were teenagers when it started to turn, believe it or not." He thought it was kind of cool, to be honest.

"It looks great on you. I like it very much. Genetics are fascinating, aren't they?" Charles stepped in behind him, and the shower suddenly felt small.

"Uh-huh..." Oh, this was new.

Wonderful.

He leaned right in.

"Mm, isn't that hot water nice?" Charles caught him with one arm and kissed him while the hot water rained down on his shoulders. It was romantic and exciting, and over much too quickly.

Charles pushed him under the spray and wet his hair, then grabbed the shampoo and massaged it into his scalp while humming something that seemed familiar. He wondered if Charles ever sang in the shower.

His eyelids went heavy as Charles rubbed his scalp, fingertips digging in hard.

Charles just kept humming, using soapy fingers as he moved lower for a neck and shoulder rub. "You are...you have become quite important to me, cowboy. I want you to know that."

"I'm going to take good care of you. I swear to God." Hopefully that was going to be enough.

"I know. You already do, cowboy." Charles titled his head back and the water rained down, washing all the soap from his hair.

Lord, that felt so fine. His body responded—no hesitation, no way to hide it.

Charles squeezed out some body wash from the pumps on the wall and lathered him up—chest and abs, ass, under his balls and down the length of his prick, hands gentle but teasing. "Here I am trying to clean you up, and you're getting dirty again."

"All your fault." Mister Charlie had some amazing hands on him, and they made Ryder a little stupid.

"Well, that's going to have to wait." Charles leaned close to his ear. "Unless you want to take care of it and show me." Charles's tongue slid along his jaw, and Charles kissed him before he could answer.

He whimpered, opening up even as he reached down for his heavy prick. He knew how to get himself off in short order. He was, in fact, a master of that.

But their kiss was way hotter than most of what was in his imagination. It was real.

As the kiss ended, Charles leaned back in the shower, putting enough space between them to watch him.

His cheeks heated, but Ryder reckoned if he couldn't do this in front of his lover, he wasn't ready to have a lover.

He was so ready to have a lover.

Charles gave him a deep nod and a smile. "You're beautiful; do you feel beautiful? You should."

"I feel revved up and a little nervous." Beautiful? He didn't see that, but he thought he wasn't half bad.

"No need to be nervous, cowboy. Unless you don't want to, then you can just say so, it's okay."

"I want to. I just never have, you know?" He'd never even considered.

That earned him another smile. "Aren't firsts wonderful? They're just that. One time. You never get them back."

"Then I'd better not mess it up then, right?" He chuckled and stroked again, base to tip.

"You won't. Something tells me you've had plenty of practice." Mister Charlie's voice got deeper. "When you're done you can help me clean up too. I hope that's something else to look forward to. Maybe not as good as an orgasm, but —" He got a wink.

Oh, he didn't know. He privately loved the idea of washing Charles, making him happy and warm and comfortable. "I'm more than willing. More than."

"Thank you." Charles caught his chin and kissed him again, lingering this time, giving him plenty of heat to work with.

His hand tightened, and he dragged his palm over the tip, making his eyes cross. Fuck, he loved that little rush.

"Mm. More." Charles nipped at his chin.

"Uh...uh-huh." More worked for him. He offered Charles his throat, his abs going tight as his balls drew up.

Charles took advantage, nibbling and kissing down to his shoulder. "So hot, my beautiful cowboy." That deep voice just barely reached him over the running water and the sound of his heartbeat in his own ears.

His neck was one hot spot after the other, and he couldn't fight his moan. His hand moved faster, as he slid into second gear. He wasn't going to live here long.

"Love that sound." Charles slid wet hands over his chest, tracing muscle and teasing his nipples. "You're what I need, cowboy. You're all I need."

Ryder wasn't sure how he'd lucked into all this, but he was grateful he had. "Yes, Sir."

"Are you close? You sound close." He got another kiss, and then Charles looked down between them, staying close this time with one hand behind his back, steadying him.

"Uh-huh. Close." He licked his lips, bracing himself, his thighs spreading. "Oh, fuck me."

"Come on, Ryder. Show me how beautiful you are."

He moaned and went up on tiptoe, Charles's words sending his orgasm tearing through him in a wild rush.

"Yes. That's right." Charles pulled him in with that arm behind his back and kissed him again, barely letting him suck breaths in between.

He was dizzy and loving this, more than willing to give Charles anything he wanted.

"Mmm. Do you feel good, cowboy?" Charles let him go, and the water poured over him, rinsing him clean again.

"Uh-huh. So good." He blinked, reaching for Charles with shaking hands.

Charles turned them, stepping under the water and giving him some room to see, to touch. "I do love a shower."

"Me too." He blinked a little to focus, then he grabbed the soap, lathering his hands up. "I love this."

"I can't wait to share mine at the estate. It's enormous."

He'd seen it. It had two shower heads and seats and steam and crazy things.

"That sounds like heaven." He soaped Charles up, exploring and adoring the man's skin, lingering on the sensitive spots.

Charles looked down at his hands. "That feels very nice, but don't get me riled up. I'd rather have a nice buzz I can indulge later."

"Yes, Sir. I'll be decent, I promise." He wasn't trying to set Charles on fire, just warm him up.

"Mmm." Charles took in a deep breath and stretched as he let it out. "Good boy."

Lord have mercy, he was going to have to pull that memory out later in private, give it a good, hard looksee.

"Mmm...turn around, and I'll wash your back, massage a little."

Charles turned dutifully, bracing one hand on the shower wall. His back was wide and muscled, much less fuzzy than his front, with a little bit of hair mostly at his shoulder blades.

"Mmm…" So pretty. Ryder dug in, rubbing hard, loving on that strong back with all he had.

"Oh, you're very good at this." Charles sighed, and Ryder felt him relax. "Very nice."

He didn't bother answering; he just kept working, melting Mister Charlie the best he knew how.

Charles didn't rush him one bit, obviously appreciating what he was doing. "I'm going to need a nap if you keep that up." He was pretty sure Mister Charlie was teasing.

"Mmm…you must have needed it, then." If it felt so good, it was necessary.

"No naps for me. We have brunch soon and people to see."

"We do. I want you to get to know Roper. He's amazing."

"I have no doubt. He seemed to care about you very much when I met him yesterday. It will be nice to talk with him more." Charles turned back around. "Am I all clean?"

"You are. You're beautiful. I hope you'll let me suck you off tonight. I want your cock in my mouth."

Mister Charlie seemed pretty pleased, and heat flashed in his eyes for a second. "I am very much looking forward to that."

He found his new lover a smile. "Me too."

"Something to look forward to." Charles shut the water off and pulled him out of the shower, handing him a soft towel. "Something else."

He nodded and set to drying the beautiful body. "Something else."

Mister Charlie nodded and pulled out another towel to dry him off too. "I love how you hear me."

"It's the easiest thing ever. I listen." And he loved it.

"I know." Charles tied the towel around his waist and kissed him. "Thank you, that was very nice."

Ryder couldn't believe this. He just couldn't. He didn't even know how to process the fact that he was sleeping with Charles.

Him.

And it wasn't skeezy.

They dressed quietly, and Charles let him help with little things like buttoning his shirt for him, which gave Ryder an excuse to stay close while being helpful.

And then they were out the door for brunch.

Hand in hand.

14

————

Charles held onto Ryder's hand tighter than he probably needed to, but he had his reasons. He wanted the cowboy to know it was deliberate. He felt like he had to keep proving to himself that this was real. And for some reason, he felt the need to let people know that Ryder was his.

He was obsessing a bit over that last one, worrying it between metaphorical teeth. It was a new feeling, something he hadn't had with Tad. Perhaps because with Tad he had always been the trophy, the husband who Tad wanted to show off. He hadn't minded that. He hadn't really cared one way or another.

But he cared now.

He definitely had phone calls to make when they got back to New York. The service that'd sent Ryder, of course, to let them know he was canceling the contract, but especially to Victor. He had questions. Thoughts. Ideas.

He was beginning to understand Ryder, perhaps even on a higher level than Ryder knew himself, and he didn't want to make a mess of things.

Ryder squeezed his hand, reminding him to be present, which he certainly was not at the moment. "Should we have mimosas?"

"Orange juice and sparkly booze for the win!" Ryder seemed younger, almost carefree.

"I would agree it's a win." The hotel restaurant was busy, but the scent of hot baked goods and maple syrup was strong. "I believe we've come to the right place."

"I texted Roper. He'll be down in a few." Ryder rolled his eyes. "Don't expect him to eat. He's riding and staying lean."

Ah, yes. "Fighting weight, you explained that to me." Charles nodded, feeling like he was starting to understand this sport, for all of its insanity. "Starve yourself so you're light enough to risk your life sitting on the back of a bucking bull for eight seconds. It all sounds perfectly reasonable." He glanced at Ryder and grinned.

"You know it. Best money in the business, if you can stick and stay healthy."

"That's a big if, given what I saw last night." They were seated in a booth, and people swooped in bringing coffee, water, and a basket of breakfast pastries. He picked up his coffee. "We're going to the city after the weekend, right?"

Ryder checked his phone, then nodded. "Yes, Sir. You have meetings on Tuesday and Thursday. So you have us going to the city Sunday evening and returning to the lake house Friday morning."

"Perfect. Thank you. No more business now. Mimosas." He waved a server over and ordered, then smiled at Ryder. "Will you still keep my calendar even if you don't work for me?"

"Yes. I don't want anyone else taking care of you like I do. It's important."

Important. Ryder used that word often for things that

mattered to him, and it was clear that he wanted to keep his job without calling it work.

"It is important. I trust you, and I can't say that about too many people. I won't hire anyone, I promise."

"I've got your back. I swear to God." Ryder winked at him. "I won't let you down."

"I know, cowboy." He wanted to tell Ryder that this was bigger than letting him down, but in some ways, for Ryder, it wasn't, and he understood that. He wasn't sure why, but it seemed to fit.

Ryder beamed at him, offering him the breadbasket to choose from.

He plucked a biscuit out of the basket and reached for the butter, hungrier than he'd expected to be. That was probably because of all that exercise he'd gotten the night before.

He allowed himself a private bit of smug pleasure over that.

He'd made his cowboy ache for him, and soon he'd been in that tight body, once he found condoms and lube.

That would be one of today's errands. He didn't plan on waiting until they got to New York; he knew he couldn't make it that long. "What are you going to eat, do you think? Should we order some fruit or something for Roper?"

"I'll get him an egg white omelet with tomatoes and spinach. I'm thinking waffles. Crunchy, syrupy goodness."

"I am famished. I am going to have pancakes with a fried egg and sausage." And he might have seconds if it didn't make Roper uncomfortable.

"Sounds good to me." Ryder smiled at him, shook his head. "I hate egg whites. I had them for ten years, every damn morning. Hate them."

He had to laugh. "You cowboys really sell your souls to

this sport. I understand that plenty of athletes do—Olympic gymnasts, NBA players, marathon runners, etcetera—but I couldn't imagine never eating a full egg." He shook his head. He was much too lazy.

"Well, it's only for twenty years, if you're super lucky. Most of us, it's for ten or so." Ryder wasn't being facetious. He was serious as a heart attack.

Charles wasn't going to pretend to understand, but he also didn't want to insult anyone by saying so. Fortunately, he was saved by the appearance of the server, who refilled their coffees.

"I think we'd like to order please."

"Absolutely." The server was smiling at Ryder as if she knew a secret. "What can I get you?"

"I'd like waffles and a side of crispy bacon."

"I can do that, and you?" She looked Charles up and down as if she were measuring him.

"Pancakes with a side of sausage and a fried egg, please. Lots of syrup. And...and egg white omelet with...spinach and tomato, right?" He glanced at Ryder.

"Yes, Sir. That's for my brother. He'll be down in a bit." Ryder offered the server a warm smile, and she beamed at him.

"I'm on it." The server turned around and he was pretty sure he heard her say, "I love this time of year."

Ryder's chuckles were soft and amused. "Me too. I get to show off who I used to be."

"Not right now. Now, you're showing off who you are." Charles reached across the table and touched his fingers.

Ryder blinked at him, cheeks going bright pink, beaming over. "I—that sounds good."

Charles nodded to him. He didn't want to cause a scene while they ate so he did pull his hand back, but only for now, and only because they were expecting Roper. "You should be proud of who you are, always. Who you were is part of that, but it's not everything."

"I'm learning that. It's one hell of a lesson, but I am learning it."

"Then I will have to remind you often." He added cream to his coffee and picked it up to take a sip. "Not exactly gourmet, but it will serve its purpose."

"Coffee is good; good coffee is better?" Ryder winked and sweetened his cup.

"Indeed." His stomach growled, and he reached for another biscuit. "What time is the show tonight?"

"Starts at seven. Then Sunday starts at two p.m."

"Good. That gives us lots of time to wander and relax. We must try different adult milkshakes tonight." He was starting to wonder if Roper really was going to join them, or if he'd found something better to do with his time. Not that he intended to ask Ryder.

"Waffles?" A young man with arms full of food stopped next to their table.

He pointed to Ryder. "Right there. Pancakes here."

"And the egg whites are mine. Sorry, y'all. I was putting on my smell good. Hey, Ry. How goes?"

"Good. Good, have a sit."

"Good morning. Excellent timing, Roper." He took another sip of his coffee wondering what it must be like to be someone like Roper.

"It's a knack. Morning glories. Did y'all have a good night?"

Ryder blushed and smiled. "We did. You?"

"Had some whiskey at the afterparty, fell into bed, and crashed like a good little cowboy." Those eyes were wicked, challenging, so unlike Ryder's.

"You'll appreciate a little food in your stomach then, I'd imagine." He was hungry, and although he felt badly eating a full meal when Roper was restricted, it wasn't enough to prevent him from diving right in.

"Yeah. Man, give me a bite of waffle?" Roper turned those eyes on Ryder, and Ryder forked up a bite immediately.

He could see how Roper might have depended on Ryder when they rode together. No wonder Ryder got such satisfaction out of looking after him. It did seem like Roper had figured it out on his own, but the men did look happy together.

His first bite of pancakes only made him more hungry. They were sweet and spongy, very well cooked, but he probably would have eaten them even if they'd tasted like cardboard with syrup on them.

"So...you left early..."

"I told you. I'm fine. It's weird not pulling your rope," Ryder answered, and Roper shook his head.

"No. What if you fell? What if you hit your head? No."

He didn't hear the twin telepathy part of the conversation, but he didn't need to. He understood. "Your brother is right," he offered, and picked up his coffee. It didn't matter that he hadn't indicated which brother he was speaking to either. They understood. He expected that to be the end of that.

Ryder sighed softly, but he nodded. Roper shot him a grateful smile, digging into his eggs.

Charles refrained from pointing out that Ryder had other responsibilities now—to him, chiefly—he assumed that was either already clear to Roper or would be soon enough without his input.

"How are the waffles?"

"Exceptional." The twins spoke together.

Ryder added, "Thank you, Sir."

He chuckled at them both and gave Ryder a slight nod. "My pancakes are delicious, but they're disappearing so fast I question whether I'm actually tasting them or just making that part up."

"Oh, are you starving your guy, Ry? You know you got to keep him well-fed…"

"Oh, decidedly not. Ryder is an excellent cook. Very creative and capable. We just…missed dinner last night."

Roper's eyebrow flew up. "Did you?"

"Yep. Early night in. We're hungry." Ryder popped a bite of waffle in his mouth.

He caught the look Roper shot him and realized that Roper might have just come to the conclusion that Ryder was being taken advantage of.

Understandable under the circumstances, and he was relieved that he'd been up-front about that issue with Ryder.

"Ryder, perhaps you ought to explain to your brother that you are no longer in my employ?"

"He fired you?" Roper's eyes narrowed.

Ryder shook his head. "No. No. I quit. It was mutual. We wanted to be together, huh?"

He caught Roper's gaze deliberately. "I told him he had a choice. He made it. I certainly had no intention of starting something with a man who works for me. But we both wanted…to start something."

"You got a nest egg, though, right? You are good, because—"

"Solid as a rock, brother." There was no hesitation, no tension in Ryder at all.

Charles was touched by the trust Ryder had in him. He knew two things for certain. He and Ryder were going to be good for each other, and Roper would most assuredly kick his ass if he didn't treat Ryder with the respect he deserved. Ryder had chosen, however, not to share their financial agreement should things not work out between them, so he wouldn't either.

"You know your own brain, man. You're happy?"

"Yeah."

"I can visit and see where you're living? Can I tell Mom?"

Ryder glanced at him, really quickly.

That was an easy question to answer, even if it made him a bit uneasy. He couldn't be sure Ryder's family would find him suitable. "It's your home too now; invite anyone you like. And I look forward to meeting your mother."

"So, yes, you can visit, and I'll tell the family. No bringing them with you, or I will be real put out."

He kept eating and let the brothers talk. He was learning a great deal by keeping his mouth shut until spoken to.

"I would never." Roper looked shocked by the idea, but even he could tell it was a playful lie.

"Butthead. I'm serious. I'm not ready for Momma."

"Fair enough. I wouldn't be either. Ever."

The brothers grinned at each other, then started laughing, shoulder to shoulder.

As Charles watched the two of them laughing together, he realized without any resentment whatsoever that he could never be the most important person in Ryder's life. A very close second was a good possibility, but a bond like that was just different. It was important, and he knew he had to respect that.

Besides, he enjoyed seeing Ryder so happy.

"I take your mother is a lot of company?" He smiled at them and sipped his coffee.

"Mom is a lot of...woman. She's dear and brave, but she's

raised two sets of twin cowboys." Ryder winked at him. "She's bulletproof."

"Ah. Delaying a visit seems to be the prudent choice, then." He chuckled and licked coffee off his lip.

"Yeah, Mom can be intense, and with new relationship energy?" Roper shook his head, so dramatic. "Nope."

New relationship energy. He liked that. He was enjoying the energy so far, and he could see not wanting to share that with Mom.

"I'm looking forward to watching you ride again tonight, Roper."

"Thanks, man. I appreciate it. Hopefully I stick for the eight." Roper winked at him.

"I have every confidence." He gave Roper a nod and forked up a big bite of eggs. They were very edible for a hotel restaurant.

"I like him. I like him a lot. You can hang with him."

Ryder rolled his eyes. "Thanks. I live for your permission."

He chuckled and kept eating, but quietly he was pleased to be on Roper's good side. "What are your plans today? I think Ryder was hoping to spend some time with you."

"I've got nothing all day. I have to sign autographs at six, just like always."

He nodded, mouth full of another bite of maple syrup heaven. After he'd swallowed, he looked at Ryder. "I won't be the least bit insulted if you'd like some family time."

"I thought we could all do something, even if it's just gambling or bowling or something."

"Oh, do you bowl, Charles?" Roper's eyes lit up.

"Not in quite some time, but I have, yes." He was terrible at it, but he recalled having fun. "Is this something the two of you do well?"

Ryder chuckled softly. "No one said we did it well…"

He glanced up and grinned at Ryder. "Then I think we'll have a fair competition."

"We really just like throwing the ball and laughing. The place here? Does glow in the dark bowling." Roper grinned. "Let's do that."

"Glow in the dark?" That sounded dangerous, but the entire point of this adventure was to do new things. "I'm interested."

"See, I knew I liked him. Seriously." Roper winked at Ryder. "This is really a good omelet, believe it or not."

"I have no complaints about my pancakes." He had just taken the last bite. "And the coffee is drinkable."

"Isn't all coffee drinkable?" Roper asked, and Ryder shook his head.

"Not yours, man. You make terrible coffee."

He raised an eyebrow at Roper. "The coffee Ryder makes me at home is delicious. Do you make it differently?"

"We must," Ryder said. "Because Roper's sucks."

He snorted. "Noted. House rule number one. Roper is welcome in our home, but he is not to touch the coffee maker."

"Exactly. It would never be the same. Ever." Ryder caught the napkin Roper threw at him.

"Boys, we're in polite company," he teased. "Behave yourselves."

"Yes, Sir," they spoke, in perfect unison.

His lips twitched as he held back a grin. "Very nice."

They both reached for their coffee cups, said, "Thank you," and drank.

"That was cute. I can still tell you apart, though." It wasn't their looks; it was something in Ryder's eyes, in the way that Ryder looked at him. Their eyes were built the same way, but they didn't *see* the same.

Ryder watched him with weight, with intent. It was more than desire, and Charles craved it.

Roper sighed. "You'd be the only one. Except Mackey."

"It's true, though. I can tell." He winked at Roper and put his fork down. "I am stuffed."

"You made a dent." Ryder winked at him, eyebrows waggling.

"A good one. I won't need lunch." He snorted. "I'll need a milkshake later, however." Those were a worthwhile indulgence.

"Those are better than sex," Roper said, and Ryder's lips twisted.

He chuckled. Roper really was an instigator. "I'm not sure about that, but they're just as sinful."

"Sinful sex...now that's a thought."

"Roper, you be nice," Ryder muttered. "No baiting my man."

"I'm very difficult to bait. Or ruffle. Not to worry, cowboy." He reached across the table again, and took Ryder's hand, lifting it to kiss the back.

Ryder pinked, and Roper arched one eyebrow. "Y'all are sweet. Lord have mercy."

"Thank you." He let Ryder's hand go, then reached for his wallet. "I hope to keep your brother happy and... fulfilled." He chose that word carefully, curious to see if Roper would pick up on his meaning.

"You might make it. You seem to have the...vibe."

That seemed to be the acknowledgement he was looking for. "I might at that." He handed his card to the server to pay for breakfast. "So, bowling, then?"

"Sounds good to me. Thanks for breakfast." Roper held

his hand out to shake, and that tattoo of a rope with a lock peeked out.

"Yes, thank you, Sir. I appreciate it."

He shook with Roper, looking Ryder's twin right in the eyes, then signed the check and stood, putting his card back in his wallet. "My pleasure."

Roper smiled at him, then at Ryder. "Are you going to be busy tonight? Joe Gresham is coming to the show, and I have a meeting with him at the bar after."

Ryder tilted his head. "Yeah? You still working the deal, there?"

"He wants you too."

"I don't want to."

"It won't hurt—"

Ryder frowned. "I don't want to."

"Just pictures, no film? Just come talk to him. It's a lot of money."

"What's this about?" Charles took Ryder's hand. He didn't like the sound of it, and Ryder had already said no.

"I have a guy who wants cowboy twins in his commercials and ads. He wants us," Roper explained. "Both of us."

"Ah. Well, I'm sure he can find someone else." Any set of twins could dress up like cowboys after all.

"But if we do just print ads?"

Ryder sighed. "I'll meet with him, *if* Charles can come too."

He shrugged and looked at Roper. "Fair?"

"Sure. Perfect. I'll let him know. It's not a big deal, Ry. I swear."

Ryder simply shrugged.

That was a conversation he'd have with Ryder at dinner,

while Roper was signing his autographs. He needed to know everything, so he could protect his…lover.

"If it pays well, it's probably a big deal, Roper. We can let Ryder decide that for himself later with no pressure, right?"

"Sure. Sure. Joe's a decent sort. He just is…intense."

Ryder shook his head. "Bowling? Or are we going to walk and wander for a bit?"

That was strangely curt. He squeezed Ryder's fingers. "I would love to bowl; it sounds like fun. Perhaps wander later when we're tired."

"Good deal. Let's do this." Ryder smiled at him, nodded. "You know where it is, Roper?"

"I do. We're going *down*." Roper blew kisses at them.

Oh my. He had no idea what he was in for, but he was ready for the adventure.

15

———————

Ryder waved at his brother. "Good signing. We'll be there at the show."

He wanted to close his eyes and relax for two shakes.

"I'll hook up with you after the show."

"You know it." He shut the hotel room door and locked it.

Charles was sitting on the couch in the common area of their suite, and he could feel those eyes on his back. "Locking the door to keep him out or us in?"

"Both. I just needed a second to breathe, you know?" Breathe and focus.

"Come sit." Charles held out one arm and curled it around his shoulders as he sat. "That was quite a day."

"Yes, Sir. It was...busy." He leaned in, cuddling in close. Busy and a little stressful.

"It was. Roper seems to have endless energy." Charles was settled though, quiet and still.

"He does." Ryder was always a little slower to move. To breathe. To make a decision.

Charles kissed his head, nuzzling his hair. "What's on your mind, cowboy?"

He shrugged. He knew, but he didn't know if he wanted to get into it. "I'm just a little bitchy."

"Is it about the meeting tonight after the show?"

He nodded. He didn't like Gresham. Never had. There wasn't a reason. He simply didn't.

"You don't have to go just because Roper wants you to. You know I'll back you up. I'll even say no for you if you need me to." In fact, he'd wanted to do just that earlier.

"I don't want to fuck up his chance for money, but..." He didn't want to do this.

"Ryder. You don't have to do anything you don't want to do. Period. He can talk to this man himself, and if it doesn't work out for him on his own, he'll deal with that. He has to live his own life."

"It's just creepy." He turned to face Mister Charlie. "I don't like how he looks at us. It feels like porn. Roper says I'm being stupid, but—I don't like it."

"Hm." Mister Charlie sighed. "I see. So it's not just that you don't want to do it. You don't want him to do it either?"

"I wish he could see it, but...he won't." And Ryder couldn't make Roper do anything he didn't want to.

"I wondered about that myself. What can I do to help? Is being there tonight enough? Would you like me to try to talk Roper out of it?"

"Just have my back when I say no? Please? I'm retired."

Mister Charlie turned to him and caught his chin in warm fingers. "I promise. I will always have your back."

Instead of tensing, he relaxed, melting into the touch. "Thank you, Sir. I'll have yours too. I swear."

"Thank you." Mister Charlie kissed him gently. "You and I are a team now."

"I like being part of a team. It's my natural state of being." In fact, he had been born to it.

"It can be very nice. You need to be your own man too, though. You should think about what you want and what you need for yourself."

"I did. I have. You're the one I want, no question." And he knew that. The rest? He was figuring out.

Mister Charlie gave him a nod. "That makes me happy, but there is more you need to think about. More you may need. More that I can give you."

"Okay." He wasn't sure he was following, but he did know he was going to make it work.

Mister Charlie just smiled and leaned deeper into the couch. "So, bowling went better than I'd anticipated."

"I'm glad?" That was good, right? It felt right.

"Was that a question?" Charles gave him a playful look. "I won. By the skin of my teeth but numerically speaking I was the winner."

"You did! We should play again. What's your position on pool?" He was way better at that than bowling.

"I played a bit when I was younger. My family had a table in our game room, and there was one in the dormitory at college."

"I know the rules, but I'm not a shark or anything." He was best at cards or board games. He enjoyed them.

"You know me. I like cards. Poker is about as competitive as I get. Or Risk. I'm ruthless at Risk." Mister Charlie's laugh didn't really leave his chest; it just rumbled around in there.

"Oh, yes. We have fun with rummy, don't we?"

"We do. You're very good. It's nice to have some friendly competition."

"It is. It's fun to play." He loved the way they talked together, enjoyed one another during their games.

"And safer than eight seconds on a bull, for sure. How long do you think your brother will continue to ride?"

"Until he gets the injury that knocks him out of the game." Just like him.

Charles nodded. "I was afraid you were going to say that."

"It's how this works, right? We play until we can't."

"Yes, but we're not talking about your average sports injury here." Charles sighed. "I apologize; it's not as if you don't know this. But I worry for Roper."

"So do I. Every day." But that didn't matter. Not even a little bit. Roper was a cowboy.

Mister Charlie rolled his eyes. "Cowboys. I'm sorry that your career ended with such a terrifying injury, but I am very glad you're right here instead. I believe I was the winner of that show."

"I—I bet I was scared, but I sure don't remember a bit of it. I know Roper was there, and I know they called all the family, because they weren't sure I'd wake up." He'd been overwhelmed.

Charles's arm tightened around him. "How long were you out?"

"Ten days. Like I said, I don't remember it at all." It wasn't even a blur.

"Your family must have been...well. I know a little about how your family must have been. Except I knew Tad wasn't ever going to wake up."

He squeezed Charles's hand. "I'm so sorry. That had to be so very hard."

"It was at first. After a while, it was mostly very lonely. But I made him a promise, and I kept it, and I feel good about that."

"I—is it weird that I don't know what to say? Because I don't."

"No. No one really does. Nobody understood it. Sometimes even I don't, except that I'm a man of my word, and I made a promise."

"You're a good guy. I swear, you make me proud to know you."

"Thank you," Mister Charlie sighed. "I am proud to know you too."

"Thank you. I want you to be, you know." He sort of needed it.

"Mhm. Yes. I know. And I want to be the kind of man you need."

Ryder didn't think that was going to be a problem. In fact, Charles was perfect for him.

There was a knock on the door, and Charles got up like he was expecting someone. "I'll get that." A man handed Charles a bag when he answered the door, Charles gave the guy a tip and closed it. "Special delivery." The bag landed in his lap. "We needed some...provisions."

He peered inside the bag to find a bottle of lube and a box of condoms.

Charles grinned at him and sank back down onto the couch. "I had to order the M&Ms to make the delivery minimum."

Ryder couldn't stop laughing, because that was at once ridiculous and adorable and wonderful and dear.

Not to mention the hotness quotient.

Mister Charlie laughed with him. "The delivery guy gave me a thumbs up."

"He knows you're going to get lucky." He winked at his lover, a soft buzz building in the pit of his belly.

"Lucky-er. Luckier. I believe I am already quite lucky. I

have a cowboy in my bed. I've seen the movies." Mister Charlie winked at him.

"Have you? Are you suggesting I'm an archetype?" He reached up, stroking Charles's lips, loving on him.

"No. Next to you, the movies exhibit an appalling lack of imagination." Charles gently pinched one finger between his teeth.

The little sting made him gasp and scoot closer, rubbing them both together. So fucking hot.

Charles let his finger go and kissed him in that gentle, slow way he had the night before. Taking time, driving him mad.

"You make me want to hump you like a naughty puppy," Ryder confessed, his breath coming faster, harder.

"Mmm. Naughty puppy? Well, not yet, pup," Charles whispered against his lips. "Tonight, after everything. When I have time to make it just right."

"Oh, so long." He guessed that gave him something to look forward to, something to want and wait for.

"I know. It's good for us to want a little when we already know we can have whatever we desire. You will understand what I mean as the night goes on. It feels good." Charles was speaking softly, and it felt intimate, those words only for him.

He nodded, caught like a fly in a web. All he could do was listen close.

"You're used to things moving faster, I know. That can be sexy too. But first times aren't something we ever get back, and I want it to be so good for you."

"It's been a little bit." And he hadn't done that a lot anyway. Blowjobs and handjobs were less intimate.

"That makes two of us. I haven't since Tad." Charles leaned back to look at him. "I apologize. I shouldn't keep bringing him up. I don't mean to make you uncomfortable."

"You loved him. You can talk about him." It wasn't like Mister Charlie had left his husband for Ryder or something.

He got a slow nod. "I did. Thank you." Charles took a breath and straightened up. "What time do we need to be where? Because I was promised another preshow milkshake."

"Seven o'clock is when the show starts. So we can have a shake and wander, if you want. We have lots of options to explore, even the casino floor."

"Do you gamble? I've played some poker, but I don't enjoy the gambling part as much."

"I don't. Bull riding was enough, but I like to watch everyone else."

"So let's wander and drink." Charles rummaged around in the shopping bag and pulled out the M&Ms. "Peanut. My favorite."

"I know. You eat the yellow ones first, every time." Every single time.

Mister Charlie got up off the couch and offered him a hand. "I do. I love that you pay attention to the things that matter to me, and even the little things that are unimportant."

He got a quick kiss. "Come on. I'll share the yellow ones with you."

16

———

Charles led Ryder into the hotel bar by the hand. He liked holding the cowboy's hand, but he also wanted to make it very clear to whoever this ad guy was that Ryder —well, that the cowboy belonged to someone, for lack of a better phrase.

Or perhaps there was no better phrase. He felt protective right now, and along with that came a certain level of possessiveness, because he didn't intend to let anyone force Ryder into anything he didn't want to do.

Not even a twin brother, who clearly made it difficult for Ryder to refuse him.

He didn't feel as if Roper was mean or cruel, more careless, definitely reckless. Roper was the more extroverted of the two for sure and had probably gotten Ryder into many awkward situations like this one.

Hopefully not just like this one.

"Do you know who we're looking for?" Roper had headed to his room to shower and planned to meet them. "Should we just sit at the bar?"

"I know him. He'll recognize me. We can get a table, or otherwise I have to pretend to be Roper until he shows."

"All right. Pick a table and let's sit." There was no way he was going to allow Ryder to pretend to be Roper.

He examined that thought a second. Did he have the right to do that? To prevent Ryder from doing...anything? He didn't know, but then again, he supposed he could do whatever Ryder allowed *him* to do.

If Ryder needed his support in this, then he would provide it.

They found a table and sat, and he ordered them each a beer. Beer seemed to be in keeping with the evening, even if he did choose a trendy IPA for himself.

Ryder could nurse the beer as long as he wanted to.

"I'm right here," he said softly and settled his arm over the back of Ryder's chair.

"Thank you. I know it's going to be okay. I'm just going to kindly say no."

He had a bad feeling it wasn't going to be that simple, but he'd said what he needed to. He had Ryder's back.

Fans kept glancing at Ryder, frowning or smiling, then looking away when Ryder didn't respond.

"Roper?" A short man in jeans and a checkered shirt headed right for them and pulled out a chair. "How was the show? Sorry I missed it. I was doing a shoot. Is your brother coming like we talked about?"

"He is." Ryder stood with a short nod and shook the man's hand. "How goes it?"

"Good, good." The guy looked at him and stuck out a hand. "Joe Gresham."

"Charles." This guy didn't need his full name. "And this is Ryder, not Roper."

"Oh. Yeah?" Gresham laughed and took a seat. "Damn. You boys look so fucking alike."

"I've heard that a few times. Roper's on his way down. He wanted a shower."

"Now I'd pay to see that."

Ryder wrinkled his nose.

Their server brought their beer and set them on the table. "What can I get you?"

"Rum and Coke."

No please or thank you. This guy was losing his respect more and more every time he opened his mouth.

"Also four shots of Patron for the table."

Ryder shook his head. "Not for me, thanks."

"Nor I." He had Ryder's back. And he didn't care for shots in any case.

Gresham waved them off. "Four shots."

He didn't so much as twitch, but he also had no intention of even touching the shot glass when it arrived.

He was ready to leave the table with Ryder right now, but he respected that Ryder had made a promise to Roper.

He also respected that Ryder was setting his own boundaries, with his backup.

"So Roper told you what I'm looking for? He told me no video—" Gresham shook his head. "Which is a shame, but he said he thought you'd go for a photo shoot. You have a great look. He told me that's natural. The hair? Wild."

"It's just hair, but we didn't do anything to it. It's just hair." Ryder was trying to smile, but it wasn't working.

Charles looked around the bar wondering why it seemed like they were always waiting on Roper. He wondered if Ryder always had.

"It's a great look," Gresham repeated, as if "great" were the only adjective in his vocabulary.

It was entirely possible.

"Mr. Gresham—"

"Joe," Gresham waved him off again. "Please."

"Mm. Okay. *Joe*. What is it you do exactly? Roper mentioned something that sounded like marketing?"

"I make calendars, posters, that sort of thing. I'm currently making a Hot Rodeo Men calendar, and we want the twins."

"I don't..."

"Hey, y'all. How's it going?" Roper came up, beer in hand. "Sorry, but I smelled like bullshit, and I needed a bath."

Charles started to welcome Roper, but Gresham spoke up first. Or perhaps he was just louder. It was difficult to say for sure.

"Hey, man. Have a seat. We were just getting down to business. I ordered some shots."

Roper stared at Ryder, who stared back, lips tight. "Well...that's kind of you, I reckon."

Roper sat between Gresham and Ryder, the act deliberate and sure.

That made him feel much better. He picked up his beer and leaned back in his chair letting Roper handle this. *Twins*, he reminded himself. Ryder belonged to Roper first.

"So, I was just saying that the calendar I'm working on needs the two of you." Gresham leaned back as the shots arrived, then put one in front of each of them.

Ryder ignored it. "I'm retired."

"My clientele won't care. Y'all are still a fantasy. Just one photo shoot."

"Are they pictures we could show our granny?" Ryder said.

Gresham laughed. "Only if you usually skinny dip with her. Pay is good. Buy Granny a new wheelchair."

"I'm leaving. Roper?"

"What?"

"We're leaving." Ryder stood up. "Right now. We aren't doing this."

Gresham pushed a shot glass closer to Roper and leaned forward. "Half up-front, Roper. I'll take you by yourself."

"Ry—It's good money."

"I'm leaving." Ryder stared Roper down. "You make your own bed in this. I won't."

Charles set his beer down and stood with Ryder. He didn't say a word, but his stance said more than enough for Roper to understand.

Gresham didn't look the least bit ashamed of himself. "It's ridiculous money. And the fans are going to eat it up, Roper."

"Our momma will see it." Ryder stared until Roper stood.

"Sorry, man. Ryder isn't in, I'm not either."

Gresham stood as well. "Ryder's old news, Roper. He's washed up. You're the celebrity now. Don't let him ruin this opportunity for you."

Roper tilted his head and blinked like a lizard. "Pardon me? Are you insulting my brother?"

Ryder whispered, "Oh, shit."

Charles thought about stepping in and cooling things down, but they were on cowboy turf right now, and he had no intention of stepping into something he knew nothing about. This wasn't his milieu.

Fortunately, Gresham seemed to realize his mistake. "Now, Roper. I'm just telling you that you have a fan base now, and you should cash in on it."

"And I'm telling you no."

The twins stood side-by-side, and Charles knew without a shadow of a doubt they could tear this photographer into tiny pieces.

Gresham nodded, admitting defeat with his body language. "I hear you. It's a shame, but I hear you."

"Come on, Roper. Let's go." Ryder met his eyes. "Charles? You coming?"

"Yes." The look in Ryder's eyes was smoking hot. This was a bull rider he was looking at, and the side of Ryder that had taken care of Roper for so long. "Right behind you."

"Good deal." The twins stormed out, keeping him caught between them.

They had to make quite a picture, the tall Yankee flanked by twin cowboys, but he was only focused on one of them.

"I'm going upstairs, Bubba. I've got a guy on speed dial that...you know."

Ryder glanced at Roper. "You pissed?"

"A little, but mostly at him."

"'kay. Call me in the morning."

"Good night, Roper." He gave Roper a nod and took Ryder's hand. "Is he okay?"

"He'll be fine. He's going to have loud, crazy sex." Ryder rolled his eyes.

"Sounds like a great idea. Minus the crazy part." There was no way he'd ever confuse Ryder with his brother. Not if he could see into their eyes. "Let's go upstairs."

"Yes. I need—" Ryder swallowed and squeezed his hand. "You. I need you."

He heard that, and he rewarded his cowboy with his own truth. "I need you too." He hadn't needed anyone as fully and completely in his life.

He made sure Roper had already gone on his way and led Ryder to the elevators. They were still holding hands, and the heat between them was making their palms a little slippery. He made himself breathe because he was tempted to lock the hotel room door and take his lover right there. He'd promised Ryder something unforgettable, and they could build up to it—there was always time for that—but he was determined to make sure Ryder knew he wanted more.

He wanted to give his cowboy more as well.

"I was going to kick that bastard's butt. Roper was right there with me. I'm glad you were there."

"I'm not sure my presence was as helpful as it could have been. I was going to let you." He dropped his voice lower. "You're sexy when you're angry."

Ryder blew out a hard, short breath. "Then I must be goddamn irresistible right now."

No question. "Absolutely. I'm impatiently waiting to get my hands on you."

"I want that. I want you to make me blind to anyone but you."

Charles could do that. It was exactly what he wanted.

They stood close as the elevator doors shut, and he didn't even trust himself to speak, much less touch Ryder. Anywhere.

But as soon as they reached their hotel room, he fished his keycard out of his wallet and leaned close enough that Ryder knew he was right there. "In a minute, I'm going to be your whole world."

"Good." Ryder was still frowning, eyebrows drawn in close.

He opened the door and, after Ryder marched inside, he closed it and turned the lock. "Bedroom." He hadn't intended to growl.

He loved the dark, hungry look he got from Ryder, though, the way Ryder wet his lips. He followed, watching Ryder's determined stride, focused on his cowboy.

They hadn't gotten two steps into the bedroom when he reached for Ryder and pulled him in close, kissing him hard.

Ryder grabbed his ass with both hands, meeting him halfway with a deep rumble as he dragged them together.

Ryder might have rolled his eyes at his twin running off for wild sex but, in this, Ryder seemed more like Roper than not. He knew the cowboy was angry, but he didn't want that energy in their bed.

He needed to change the narrative a little.

He grabbed Ryder's wrists and pulled them away from his ass, holding on tight. "You're mine right now, cowboy. This is my room. Nobody else belongs here."

"What?" He got an utterly confused glance. "I don't understand."

"You're angry, and I sympathize. I want to make sure you're leaving that at the door."

Ryder stepped back, sighed. "Oh. Oh, right. I—Maybe I should take a shower before we get busy."

He eased up on Ryder's wrists and curled an arm around the cowboy's back. "Maybe we can start this with a shower together."

"Sure. Totally." Ryder sat in the chair and started toeing off his boots.

"Have I hurt your feelings? I want you, Ryder. Absolutely. And I want us to be present with each other."

"No. No, I'm just..." Ryder sucked in a breath, then let it out. "Ramped up. I'm just really ramped up."

"I know, and I don't mind. But I want you ramped up over me. So let me do what I promised and make sure I'm all you're thinking about." He toed off his shoes and tugged his shirt over his head.

Ryder stripped down, carefully hanging his dress shirt and jeans, undershirt, briefs and socks stowed away.

He wished he understood better what Ryder needed. He had this awful feeling that he wasn't doing enough right now. "You handled yourself so well tonight. You stood your ground, you helped your brother make a good decision, and you didn't rip that awful man's head off. I can see that it wasn't easy for you. I'm proud of you."

"Thank you, Sir. It wasn't. He's a skeeze, but it's done now."

"It is. It's done. And now we can enjoy each other." He caught Ryder's chin in his fingers and tried a smile. "Unless you'd rather finish the M&Ms instead."

"No. We can finish the M&Ms after we both shoot."

"I like it." He undressed, enjoying letting Ryder help as he pleased. They made their way to the shower, which was a decent size, though nothing like what he had at the estate.

He turned on the water while Ryder made sure there were towels in easy reach. "No shooting in the shower," he teased as they stepped in. That might be a tall order, they were both buzzing hard.

"No? Darn it." He got a wink, and he could almost see Ryder relax.

He was aware that he put a stop to what could have been some heated and satisfying sex. He enjoyed that kind of thing under the right circumstances, and they'd get there again at some point, he was sure of it.

But Ryder trusted him and was letting everything go right before his eyes, and it was beautiful, and equally satisfying in another way.

Ryder leaned under the spray, fingers sliding over his skin and making Charles shiver.

He liked Ryder's hands; they were curious and careful. "I love how you touch me."

"I like being able to touch. You have a fine body." It didn't sound like an empty compliment.

Ryder still looked like he could get on a bull tomorrow. "Thank you. Your abs are like concrete." He slid a hand over them, appreciating the ridges.

Ryder flexed for him, belly rolling so well that his fingers got caught for a second.

It was difficult to grasp that someone this beautiful, and this compatible, had just fallen into his path. He took a kiss, wanting more connection. The hot water was soothing his soul, but his body needed so much more.

Ryder was right there with him, kissing him slow and easy, letting things heat in a steady stream.

He placed a hand on Ryder's chest and pressed him against the shower wall as their kiss grew deeper and hungrier. He ached in the best way but made himself be patient a little longer. Ryder's cock, which had been flagging, began to fill for him, swelling and nudging his lower belly. It made Charles smile, that hunger, the way Ryder gave him what he needed.

He'd meant what he'd said about being Ryder's whole world. He wanted everything Ryder could see and Ryder's every thought to be of him. He wasn't selfish, and he'd make sure Ryder got absolutely everything he needed—all of himself in return.

He straightened up, and their hips met, cocks sliding together, and neither of them fought the urge to press closer.

"Think this is gonna become my favorite thing, ever," Ryder murmured. "Showering with you."

It did seem to do them both some good. "It's lovely, isn't it?" The heat and the steam set the mood, but they could get clean together later too. "We can't stay here forever, though. I have plans for us."

Ryder gave him a wicked little grin. "Do you, now? I do like...plans."

"Mhm. I'll give you three guesses, and the first two don't count." He shut the water off and reached for their towels.

Ryder was absolutely, one hundred percent focused on him, eyes watching him like a hawk.

He wrapped one towel around his waist mostly to get it out of his hands, then spent a little time toweling his cowboy off. "This is really just so we don't get the bed all wet." And it let him keep touching and keep his lover warm.

"You're spoiling me. I thought that was my job."

"I suppose it is your job, but it's absolutely my pleasure. And remember, we're just us this weekend? You insisted." He winked at Ryder, dropped the towel he was holding on the floor and unwrapped his.

"Mmhmm. You fired me. Now I'm just yours, all the time." Ryder cupped his balls and rolled them, playing with him.

That made his toes curl, and he sucked in a breath. "That's right. All the time." He took a step, backing Ryder toward the bathroom door. "You don't know how much I want you."

"Show me?" Oh, that was...those two words, mixed with the way Ryder stared at him, made his heart pound.

"Uh-huh." Charles looped an arm behind Ryder, lifting him slightly off his feet and set the cowboy down next to the bed. He was out of words, and he didn't think it mattered.

Nothing he could say would tell Ryder as much as his hands could.

As his kiss could.

As his cock could.

Ryder crawled up onto the bed, kneeling up tall, hands holding his head as they devoured one another.

He caught Ryder's prick in his hand and stroked it slowly as they kissed. It was silky to the touch, warm and hard under the soft skin, and a little damp at the tip, enough that he could work it around with his thumb.

Ryder's kiss began to get more heated, more hungry, the need obvious as hell.

They didn't need to work up to anything; they were both already there. He pushed Ryder over, and he landed on his back among the pillows. He reached out his longer arms and grabbed the lube, tossing it next to Ryder.

Opening the box of condoms felt strange. He and Tad had never used them, and he was definitely out of practice.

"Is everything all right?" Ryder opened the lube, pulling the safety lid off.

He chuckled softly. "Oh, yes. I'm just an idiot. I haven't used one of these in a very long time."

"Would you like me to put it on you?"

"Mm. Sexy and helpful." Charles handed one to Ryder. He was perfectly capable of putting on a condom, but Ryder liked helping, making things easier for him. And yes, the whole idea was hot besides.

Ryder opened the package and eased the condom over his cock, smoothing it down, fingers moving slowly over his shaft. That steady touch was maddening, and it was all he could do not to thrust into those hot hands. He looked between Ryder's hands on his prick and the look of concentration on Ryder's face, unsure which was more of a turn on.

He put a little pressure on Ryder's knees, and the cowboy opened for him, then he picked up the lube and poured some on his fingers. "Just warming this up for you."

God, he sounded like he'd been swallowing gravel.

"Mmhmm… I can't wait to feel your cock inside me." Ryder's cock was bobbing over his belly, and his thighs were trembling under his touch.

"Soon, *pup*." He winked at Ryder and dropped a hand between them, slick fingers gliding lightly over the cowboy's ass. Keeping his self-control now would be a challenge, but Ryder deserved a slow, steady hand.

Ryder groaned, a dark, dull flush climbing up that perfect belly. "I'm so ramped up it's like I'm fixin' to ride."

"You can if you like. Next time." He added pressure with one finger and it slid up against Ryder's tight little muscle so he worked that spot with the lube and more pressure until Ryder started to relax. "That's it, I need to get you ready for me, cowboy."

Ryder nodded slowly. "Been a while. So glad it's you."

He nodded, because otherwise he'd probably grunt or something. But it had been a long while for him too, and he hadn't imagined he'd ever be with anyone he cared about like this again.

He added a second finger, and his cock leapt at the gentle stretch, making him moan. "We're going to be so good together. I know it."

"Uh-huh. Please. Don't stop, okay?"

"I won't." He wasn't going to stop unless Ryder changed his mind, and that didn't seem likely given how the cowboy's whole body was flushed and ready for him. He pressed his fingers deeper and twisted them slowly.

"Please..." Ryder rocked down, trying to take more.

Needy boy.

He let Ryder drive a little, giving his lover more until his fingers were flush against that sweet ass. Then he pulled back and added a third finger, watching Ryder's face and admiring that pretty grimace.

"I—damn, love. I feel that deep inside." Ryder's voice had gone husky, rough and raw.

"Fuck." His patience was at an end. Charles pulled his fingers back and caught his aching cock in his fist. "I want you feeling me."

"Yes. Fuck yes. Please." Ryder tugged one leg up and out, spreading wide.

If that wasn't consent, he didn't know what was. He lined up, his prick twitching impatiently in his fist, and moved over Ryder and rocked his hips, breaching his cowboy nice and slow.

Maddeningly fucking slow.

Ryder's lips parted, his eyes rolling back in his head. It was beautiful, the way need was painted on Ryder's face.

Charles took a breath and continued with care, even though his balls were screaming at him. He needed to be sure Ryder was okay, that his lover was ready for more.

"Mister Charlie. Love. *Please*."

That was what he had needed.

He blinked for just a second at the nickname and that lovely four-letter word, but he couldn't focus on either. They were overshadowed for the moment by the word "please." He gave in, hips pressing up against Ryder's ass for just a second before his need took over. He wanted to say something in return, but everything came back to, "God, you feel so fucking good."

"Yes!" Ryder bucked up, driving up toward him, taking his cock to the root.

He braced himself near Ryder's head and let go, hips driving hard, taking what he needed. His thighs were tight, and his balls pulled up, and he shifted to wrap one hand around Ryder's cock. He was too fucking close, Ryder needed to come along on this ride.

Ryder bared his teeth, his entire body gripping Charles's cock like a fist, milking his prick.

Ryder was so beautiful, even more than usual, if that was possible. He tried to focus on Ryder—working the cowboy's erection through his fingers, keeping up a steady pace—and not on his own orgasm, which was threatening to overwhelm him. "Fucking gorgeous, cowboy."

"Close. So close. So close." Ryder panted, lips parted, chest heaving.

"You, then me." He wanted to feel Ryder's orgasm around his cock. Then he'd let himself go.

"Uhn."

Charles assumed that was a yes, because Ryder's body clenched, and he shot, spunk pouring over Charles's fingers.

Ryder was so pretty when he came, the cowboy's expression somewhere between sweet agony and pure bliss. He looked down between them as his fingers slipped along Ryder's length and groaned, then braced himself as his need took over, commanding the moment, sending him deeper and harder into his lover.

"Yes..." Ryder whispered. "I'm yours."

"Mine," he replied with a growl, right on the edge. He buried himself in Ryder as he shot, holding himself there and rocking gently through it until he could get a breath. He used it to whisper, "Mine," then took a deep kiss because words weren't easy or enough.

Ryder opened up to him, offering himself up, nice and easy.

His arms started to tremble as that deep, satisfied kind of exhaustion set in and he rolled off Ryder, sinking like a stone into the pillows. He started to protest the gentle fingers on his prick until he realized Ryder was once again dealing with the condom for him.

So sweet, how the cowboy took care of him.

Ryder cleaned him up, tucked him in, and then cuddled in next to him.

"Come here." He pulled Ryder in close and kissed him. "Thank you."

"You're something special, I swear." Ryder licked his bottom lip, humming low.

"You're unlike anyone I've known. You're unique. Beautiful." And that was tangled up with complicated emotions he wasn't looking very carefully at tonight.

He needed to talk to a friend. A peer. Someone like River or Victor who could explain...all of this to him and help him process it.

Tonight was for Ryder though. He had his arms full and he was happy.

He just needed to hold on tight.

17

They were back in New York City, and it was all right with Ryder. He liked the lake house best, but this little apartment—big apartment—was fascinating, and he had a ball exploring neighborhoods, going places with Charles. There was always something neat to do, somewhere new to eat, some new food to try. A museum here, a park there.

So, yeah, he liked the lake house better because Mister Charlie was less busy, and they spent a lot more time making love or playing cards or reading. Sitting together. He'd even gotten Charles to watch a couple of movies with him.

But he didn't hate being in the city.

Charles was out at the meeting, visiting some clients, and Ryder had made an appointment to get his hair cut, pick up dry cleaning, grab Mister Charlie some of his favorite pastries, that sort of thing.

They'd arranged to meet at this private club. He guessed it was mostly a bar, because they were going to go to supper afterward. They were going to meet there at six o'clock, have a drink, and then go have Greek food.

He got on his good jeans and a decent shirt, plus a light jacket. It was drizzling, and he thought he'd need it. He hoped Mister Charlie had remembered him an umbrella.

Ryder frowned and grabbed one, just in case. He'd hate for Charles to catch a chill.

He headed downstairs a little early because Mister Charlie had said that the car would just pick him up there at their building. He felt a little high hat about everything, but he didn't know about the subway. There was something about being under the ground that just kind of wigged him right the fuck out.

He didn't know if he wanted to do that. Especially not by himself.

That was one of his things, one of his deepest-held secrets. He wasn't so good by himself. He'd never been by himself, so he didn't know what to do with it. He was great for a few hours, sure, but he was meant to be part of a team. He had been conceived as a part of a team.

So he'd just go down, chat with the security guy and the doorman and wait for his car.

Easy peasy lemon squeezy.

A text came in with Mister Charlie's chime, and he pulled out his phone. It was a big fat paragraph with perfect punctuation. He'd have known it was Charles even without the custom chime.

CHARLES

Hello, Ryder. Unfortunately, my meeting is
running overtime, and I am going to be late
for our drink. You should go ahead without
me and have a beer. River and Kacey will be
there. Do you remember them from Victor's
party? Go relax, and I'll join you as soon as
I can.

RYDER

All right. I don't need a...card or anything?

He'd only been to a few private clubs.

CHARLES

I'm told we will have a tab already in place.
If it's a problem, I'll pay when I arrive. I'm
sorry about this.

RYDER

No. I'm good. No stress

He'd meant some way to get into a private club. He was
just random Joe Number One.

Maybe there was a public place to hang out to wait for
Charles, if he couldn't get in.

The car pulled up just as he was about to say hi to the
doorman, and the driver got out and opened a door for him.
"Mr. Vales? I'm here to pick you up."

"Hey there, Alan! How's it going?" He waved and smiled.
"And it's Ryder, man. I'm not a mister."

"Mr. Ryder then." Alan winked at him. "You're looking
good. Not so skinny."

"Thanks. There's so much to eat and explore here." He
loved how there was all this stuff to learn.

Alan closed the car door after he got in. "I don't know

what you're doing, but Mr. Martin has been in a very good mood this visit."

"Excellent. That's my whole goal." He wanted to make Charles happy.

"Well, you're achieving it. It's nice to see. He was always so...quiet."

"Thanks." He settled in the car, then leaned forward. "Have you ever been to the club I'm heading to?"

"I've driven there before. I've never been inside. It's a men's club. Lots of leather."

"Ah." A men's club. "Cool."

He texted Roper.

RYDER

going to a 'mens club'. Charlie not here yet. DO I NEED A SECRET PSWD?

Roper's reply came back right away.

ROPER

YES IT'S PEANUT BUTTER!

RYDER

Don't b a dick. Should I wait outside???

He didn't want to be turned away.

ROPER

Do whatever he told you to do. If he told you to go in, then they're expecting you. Call everyone Sir. Be charming.

RYDER

I'm always polite but ok. I'll go in. This is weird.

ROPER

Nah. You're fine. Breathe.

RYDER

Breathing. On it

It was a short trip, and Alan hopped out to open his door for him again. "Mr. Martin just texted me, and he asked me to walk you to the door."

"Oh? That's kind. Are you sure?" He smiled at Alan, feeling better already.

"Of course. Ready?" Alan closed the door after he got out.

"I am. Thank you for this. I appreciate it."

"No problem." Alan smiled at him and led the way.

The door opened and a man in leather pants, big boots, and a dark vest held it for them.

"Hello. We're looking for Master River?" Alan seemed completely relaxed. "I'm Alan. This is Ryder, he's expecting us."

"Of course. Welcome, Ryder. Have a seat at the bar."

Alan smiled at him. "All good?"

"Yes. Thank you. You were very kind." Going up to the bar was something he completely understood.

"It's nice in here, huh? Fancy." Alan pulled out a barstool for him.

"Yeah. It's gorgeous. I can see why Charles likes it. He's the finest man I've ever known."

Alan gave him a sidelong glance and a knowing grin. "I feel like maybe the terms of your employment have changed recently."

"Yes. I'm not employed by Charles. I'm *with* Charles." And he wasn't going to hide that, not for a second.

Alan turned all the way this time to face him, smiling wide. "Oh my God. He is so lucky. That is amazing news."

"It is. I'm so happy, man. Seriously. He's amazing, and I love him." In fact, he was a little stupid in love.

"I've worked for him since a few years before his husband's accident, and he—he kind of disappeared. But he's coming back. I noticed how chatty he was with you, and he'd be taking you out. It's good. You're good for him."

He loved hearing that. He wanted to be a good thing in his lover's life. He wanted to be the best thing.

"Ryder! It's good to see you again. Welcome home." River, the big guy he'd met at that first party headed toward him, with Kacey behind him. At least he thought that was Kacey. River was in full leather and seemed even bigger than before. "Master Charles let me know you were going to be late. We thought you and Kacey could hang out for a while until he gets here."

"Thank you." Right, call everyone Sir. "Thank you, Sir. I was a little unsure if there was a membership card or something."

River chuckled. "Master Charles isn't a member; he's my guest tonight. And s—you don't need a membership."

Kacey slid out from behind River. He was in jeans and a gauzy, near see-through shirt and looked great.

Alan slid off his stool and offered it to Kacey. "I think you're in good hands, Ryder. Good talking to you. I'll pick you and Mr. Martin up later."

"Thank you, Alan." River gave Alan a nod, and Alan turned and left.

Kacey bumped shoulders with him. "Hey, man. What do you want to drink?"

"I think I'd like a beer—whatever's on draught. I like your shirt. How have you been?"

"I'm good. Master River loves this shirt." Kacey waved the bartender over. "*Loves* it."

"What can I get you?" The bartender was bare-chested but had a thick, studded collar around his neck.

Kacey ordered their beers. "Rumor has it you've been fired. Or did you quit?" Kacey grinned at him. "Whichever one, I'm happy for you guys."

"It was six of one, a half dozen of the other." He grinned at Kacey, rolling his eyes at himself. "I'm very happy. Seriously." He was over the moon.

"You look it. You look great." Kacey looked around. "Are you...have you been to a club like this before?"

"I haven't. I've been in a lot of bars, but not one that's all guys." Not a gay bar.

"All guys is nice, you know? It's...well, it was weird for me too at first, I guess, but it's good. Once you relax—when Charles gets here—you'll like it. It's a good place."

"I'm glad y'all are here." He sipped his beer, glancing around. The bar was gorgeous—glass and lights and wood. The stools were comfortable, the music was there, but not loud.

Alan had been right—there was a lot of leather. Not on the couches like he'd thought, though. Alan had meant the men.

"If you have any questions—about anything—you can ask me. I had a lot. Sometimes I still have them." Kacey picked up his beer.

"Oh, cool. I—everyone here is queer? I mean, it's safe to be out?" It seemed fair to ask.

Kacey nodded. "Everyone here is queer. The labels vary, but they're all under the rainbow. They're also kinky, so this is the safest place you can be."

"Excellent." He had a lot of thoughts about that, but he wasn't sure he wanted to dwell on any of it.

"Are you still doing all the stuff you were doing when you were working for Charles? Or did he hire someone else?"

"I'm doing it. It's my pleasure, you know? And I want to make sure that things are done right." He was the only one who could do that.

Kacey nodded. "That's your thing, huh? That's what you give him? Your service?"

He tilted his head. He'd never thought about it that way, but it made sense, maybe. "I want to make his life good. That makes my soul at peace."

"That's cool. That you figured that out. Peace was a lot more work for me. A lot." Kacey shook his head and sipped his beer.

"I understand that." Roper was kinky. Roper had a hard time finding anything...long-term. He thought part of that was intensity, maybe? He wasn't intense. He had a bit of a temper, sure, but he wasn't all intense.

"I ended up with River because I got in a fist fight with the wrong guy." Kacey winked at him. "Or maybe it was the right guy, you know. Since it turned out good."

"He looks at you like he really cares." He meant it too. River watched Kacey like a hawk.

Kacey's cheeks heated, and he nodded. "Yeah. He does. He did long before I did. He's like that."

He smiled, glancing around. It was a little odd—there were men kneeling on the floor, there were men dancing together, there were men in all types of clothing.

It didn't seem like Mister Charlie's type of thing, but what did he know?

"Ryder." Mister Charlie's hand landed on his shoulder, and he got a kiss on his cheek. "I'm sorry I'm late. Hello, Kacey."

"Hello, Sir. I like your suit."

Charles laughed and shrugged out of his jacket. "I'm a little overdressed, hm?"

"Never. Let me take your jacket, Sir. Is there somewhere I can hang this up safely, buddy?"

Kacey grinned at him. "There is. Come on; I'll show you."

"I'll be right back," he promised, and followed Kacey to a coat check room.

———

CHARLES LOOSENED his tie and rolled up his sleeves as he watched Kacey lead Ryder off to the coat check, admiring Kacey's mesh top. He'd only been in this club a couple of times; it was private and he neither had a membership nor did he feel he needed one.

River waved at him from a table across the club, and he waved back and headed that direction. He didn't feel uncomfortable—men were men, and he actually enjoyed the diversity of relationships, but he couldn't say he felt like he belonged here either.

He had questions, though, and this was a good place for them.

River stood and shook his head. "Welcome, friend. How are you, this fine night?"

He grinned and sank into a chair. "I just came from a meeting that was entirely too long and could have been an email. Thank you for looking after Ryder for me. I was afraid he'd be overwhelmed, but he seems to be in very good hands."

"He was fine. Perhaps a little nervous." River winked at him.

"When I asked if we could talk, I hadn't immediately assumed you'd suggest we come here, but I suppose it fits with my line of thinking. Will Kacey keep Ryder entertained for a bit?" What he needed to know wasn't going to be a quick discussion.

"Yes. He understands that you and I needed to talk. He's going to stop by and ask if it's okay to show Ryder the sub's lounge."

"Perfect, thank you. What are you drinking? Can I get you another?" He needed an ice breaker.

"I'll take a Coke this time, I think. I like to keep scene nights slow."

He hopped up and went to the bar, returning quickly with a Coke for River and a whiskey for himself. He only wanted to sip it, but that first taste burned just right and gave him the courage to start talking. "I think Ryder needs... a very specific kind of care."

"I believe every sub needs a specific type of care, but, please, let me know what you mean."

Charles set his glass down and leaned forward. "When I hired him, he was sort of a personal assistant mixed with some light housekeeping duties. We've evolved beyond that formal relationship, and now he no longer works for me, but his duties haven't changed at all. He wants to continue to... take care of me. It's very important to him. Very...personal." He sighed. He wasn't sure he was doing a very good job of explaining it all.

"So he's a service sub. That's lovely. Are you getting what you need from that arrangement?"

A service sub. Interesting. "Surprisingly, yes. I hadn't thought of myself as someone who—someone who *needed* anything. But everything about Ryder sets my soul at ease."

"Then it's amazing you found one another without trying. I love that for you." River beamed at him.

It was amazing. Baffling, in a way, as well. "I worry that I don't know how to take care of him in return."

"That means you're going to make him happy, I think. Seriously though, you need to watch and make sure he's not getting burn-out. That you make sure he is letting you know his needs. Communication, communication, communication."

He snorted. "Have you ever met a cowboy? I've learned that communication is...challenging."

"Well, no one said this was going to be perfect, right?" River winked at him.

"No, I suppose not." He sighed. "Although Ryder is a perfectionist."

"That's tough. You're going to have to watch for self-flagellation. Beating himself up isn't his job, right? You get to decide if he's pleasing you."

He raised an eyebrow. That was interesting. He hadn't thought about it that way. "That makes perfect sense. But I don't want to beat him up either."

River's chuckle was low and husky. "No, but you can be the man to say 'Stop beating yourself up' or 'No, we are going to sit and relax.' Does that make sense?"

He could manage that, assuming he understood what was happening. "And that will be enough for him?"

"You'll have to talk to him about that. Can you gauge his happiness, his satisfaction very well?"

"I think I'm learning. He's not what I'd call an open book, but we're close now. Intimate. I think I can tell when he's not himself." Fortunately, Ryder was fundamentally happy. All things being equal, his cowboy was usually in a good mood.

"Then trust your gut. Tell him what you need, let him give it to you, and let his service mean something to you." River sipped his drink. "It's a give and take."

"You make it sound easy. Of course you've had a fair amount of experience. I have one big question. How do I know if he wants to define himself as a sub? And if he does, what does that mean for me exactly? Does it need to be clearly defined?"

"It's something to discuss, for sure. Snuggle up together, turn down the lights, and have a nice, long discussion."

He'd assumed the long discussion was going to be with River. He'd hoped for the hard-earned wisdom of someone who had been in the lifestyle a while, who would give him a window into how this all works. Snuggle up and talk wasn't that. He wasn't disappointed, or worried, he just realized something he hadn't before.

"I've been thinking about this all wrong."

"This is utterly unique between the two of you. Whatever life you build together, it's yours. Your rules."

He nodded. "Which makes complete sense, of course. I don't know why I was thinking we had to fit in somehow."

"It's human nature, isn't it?"

He squinted at River. "You're much too good at this. Thank you for the advice."

"Of course. Any time. Honestly. Please remember, I'm here to help."

He took another sip of his whiskey, and it went down smoother this time, like he understood it better.

"So Kacey and Ryder are where now? The sub lounge?"

He'd bet Ryder was getting an eyeful. He was getting quite the vibe out here.

"Yes. Would you like me to text them to come back?"

"Sure. I think I'm prepared." He chuckled and shook his head. "Let's hope that's not a bad sign."

"I have faith in you, man. You've got this."

That was nice to hear. "I'm ready."

He watched as River texted, and it wasn't a minute before they appeared.

Ryder seemed more than a little shell-shocked, a little overwhelmed, and completely happy to slide in next to him.

He understood. The club could be intimidating. He'd been here several times now, but his first visit had been eye-opening.

"Hello, cowboy." He put an arm around Ryder's shoulders and kissed his hair. "Would you like to try my drink?" He slid his half a finger of whiskey in Ryder's direction.

"It smells good." Ryder sipped a little, humming deep in his chest. "Oh, that's nice."

"Isn't it? Help yourself. I can get another." Kacey started to kneel, but River shook his head and patted the chair next to him and Kacey settled there with a smile. "I was overwhelmed when I came here for the first time."

"It's something else." Ryder offered him a smile, leaning in the slightest bit. "Do you need anything, Sir?"

"Not right now. Not here." He gave Ryder a wink. They were headed back to the estate in the morning, and once they got settled, it would be time to talk. Tonight they could just relax and enjoy the company.

"Fair enough." Ryder leaned back, the colored lights shining off the silver hair.

Ryder was beautiful and smelled great. Charles had

missed the cowboy all day long. He'd ask for what he needed when they left. That was just between the two of them, after all.

Just like the conversation they needed to have, and the lifestyle they would create together.

Just between the two of them.

18

R yder was so tickled to be heading home for a few weeks. The lake house was quickly becoming his favorite place on earth.

Mister Charlie was dozing next to him, snoring softly, and Ryder was juggling his schedule a little bit, giving him more time to de-stress before supper.

It was actually Mister Charlie who'd decided they'd stay at the lake house for a while. Tomorrow, he had to make arrangements for Charles to attend some meetings by Zoom instead of in person. It seemed like they both wanted some time on their own.

It worked out like a charm, honestly, and he was tickled as hell. He wanted a chance to sit and watch the water, work on the garden, cook in the big kitchen, and drive his truck.

ROPER

Yo how was NYC?

Roper's text popped up, obscuring the calendar he was working on.

RYDER

> Weird, cool. You know. I went to the bar. It was fine

It was actually cool, if a little crazy and overwhelming. So many men. So much leather. So many piercings.

ROPER

> fine? that's it? FINE? Come on, man. Do better.

RYDER

> WHAT? Everyone was nice. Sweet. Polite.

Now he was just being a dick.

ROPER

> Sweet my kinky gay ass. Give it up, bro

RYDER

> OMG SO MANY GUYS & LEATHER & O.O

That was the best he had.

ROPER

> LOLOL Fuck, I'm DYING. I'm so fucking jealous. Can I come visit so you can take meeeee? PLEASE

RYDER

> I'll ask Charles. We're upstate for a few, but we'll go back to NYC.

He'd love that, and so would Roper.

ROPER

> I'm gonna hold you to that. So. Next question. Are you happy?

RYDER

Yeah.

He so was, and he was having a ball learning all about Charles. He'd already learned a ton, but it just seemed to get deeper every day.

ROPER

Good. Watch me on TV tonight. Gotta run

RYDER

Promise. Love you. Bye

He chuckled and put his phone away.

"Roper, hm?" Charles asked softly. "Only makes you laugh like that."

"Yeah, he wants to head down to the city with us. He wants to go to that club with us and see." He offered Mister Charlie a grin. "We're almost there."

"Mm. Good. I'm ready for a warm fire, some tea, and my slippers. Sorry I dozed off; you know me and these long drives."

"I do. I know more about you every day." Every single day, and he loved it.

"That's probably true, isn't it? I'm learning about you too. And there are some things I've been thinking about—I think they would make a nice afternoon of conversation. Do you have things you need to do today?"

"I have to unpack us, mostly. Make sure everything is nice. I was thinking soup for supper." Something easy.

"That sounds perfect. Comfort food. We're on the same page, no surprise there." Mister Charlie gave him a warm smile. He loved the way Charles looked at him, always with care and affection in his eyes.

"No surprise at all." He cupped Mister Charlie's cheek, loving on him.

"Oh, look at the trees. All those red and yellow leaves. The sun makes them look like they're on fire. I love this time of year up here. Chilly, but beautiful."

"I'm so excited to spend my first fall up here. I want to buy a neat sweater to wear around the house."

"You're going to need more than one. It gets cold and, as much as I love all the windows, they can feel a little drafty. Sweaters and wool socks and toasty slippers."

"That sounds like heaven." He rolled his eyes at himself. "Maybe not cowboy, but pure damn heaven."

Charles laughed. "Does that bother you? I could build you a little barn with some hay and a wood stove to wear your hat and boots around in if you'd like."

"Only if there's a horse to go with it." He snorted, but just a little.

Charles shrugged. "You could have a horse. You could have two horses."

"We can talk about that, absolutely. Maybe in the spring. I want to focus on us, your schedule."

Charles chuckled. "I was mostly being silly because you were lamenting that slippers weren't cowboy."

"No. They're...hygge?" Was that how he was supposed to say that?

Charles barked out a laugh. "Did you just say hygge? I've been told I'm pretentious, and even I have never managed to use hygge in actual conversation." Charles's shoulders shook. "Bravo."

He did a weird half-bow in the car seat. "Thank you. Thank you very much."

"Oh, look. Our lake." Charles took his hand. "It's good to be home."

"Our lake." How good was that? Their lake.

Charles tangled their fingers. "Well, we have to share it with a few people and some boats, but it's ours."

"That's more than fine. I like boats." And Charles. A lot.

The car pulled into the looping driveway and stopped right in front of the house.

"All right. We made it." He kissed Charles's cheek. "Welcome home, Sir."

They got their luggage into the house and Charles took his bag toward the stairs. "I'm going to change. Would you start tea?"

"Of course, Sir. I'll be up in two shakes to unpack us. Earl Grey?"

"Yes, please. With lemon." Charles headed up the stairs. "Hello, house!"

Ryder chuckled and set the kettle up. As it heated, he put out mugs, cut a lemon, found the honey, and pulled out some stew beef.

By the time he got upstairs, Charles was in soft, dark pants and was bare-chested under a lush smoking jacket. The suitcase was sitting untouched on the bed. "I could smell you coming. That lemon is fresh, hm?"

"Yes, Sir. I put some honey in too." He handed the tea over, then started unpacking their cases.

Charles took a sip, slurping a little because it was still pretty hot. "Oh, that's nice. Thank you." Charles settled in the little sitting area in the corner of the bedroom. "I'd offer to help, but I know how you are."

"I'm fine, love. I just need to get us put back to rights. You look comfy." He started sorting. The laundry room was up here, and it made things much easier.

"I am. I'm enjoying my tea. You seem eager to get us out of suitcases, and I'm not going to get in your way."

"I lived my whole adult life in suitcases." He grinned and sorted more laundry. "I like being home."

"I love it when you call this house home. I love that you feel that way, that you feel comfortable saying so. It's exactly what I want for us."

"It's an amazing place. I mean, home is you, but this is house-home." He rolled his eyes at himself. God, he was a giant dipshit.

Charles smiled and sipped his tea. "We haven't talked about the club the other night."

"We haven't. That was good whiskey. Amazing even."

"It was excellent. I enjoyed sitting and watching everyone go by. How was your talk with Kacey?"

"It was a little wild, to be honest. Some of those guys were...fascinating." And a little shocking, maybe, but nice. Everyone was nice.

"I'm sure. There was quite an array of styles and tastes. I had a good talk with River. About you."

"Me? Why?" Had he screwed something up? He didn't think so.

"Because I think it would be healthy for us to recognize our dynamic for what it is. I think you have certain needs, and I want to make sure I'm taking care of you as well as you take care of me. River confirmed what I was already thinking. He called you a service sub." Mister Charlie was watching him carefully as he spoke, eyes focused on him. "How do you feel about that?"

"I—" It sort of sounded nasty. "I don't know. Should I feel bad?"

"No. No, I wouldn't be bringing this up if I thought it was a bad thing. I look at it as a way to understand yourself, and us, better." Mister Charlie stood and walked slowly in his direction. "Let me suggest something. I have plenty of money; I can afford to pay someone to do all of the things you do for me and then we could just be together and spend our days any way we like. What would you think of that? Letting someone else take care of us?"

He shook his head immediately. "No one can do it as well as I do. I care about you, your comfort, your ease. For someone else, it's just a job."

Even when it was his job, he'd taken great care.

"I agree. I don't want anyone else. But what do you get out of that? You're not getting paid, and you're not being taken care of in the same way. Why do it?"

"You care for me in a thousand ways, but I do it because I care about you. Because I need to make life easier for you." It made him happy.

Mister Charlie smiled at him gently. "You *need* to. I understand that about you. That need isn't about me, it's about you. It's how you define yourself. That's what River meant. You do what you do because you care about me, but you need that for yourself. It's your service, your gift, your submission to me."

He wasn't sure he understood, but he wasn't sure he didn't. "But it's for you. It wouldn't be right if it was just anyone."

"Yes. Because we're a couple. But if you were on your own, the need would still be there, don't you think?"

"To have someone to take care of, you mean?" Ryder nodded, because that absolutely made sense. "Yes, Sir."

"Yes." Charles cupped his chin. "Are you starting to see what I'm saying? That's who you are. You're a service sub. You have a deeply ingrained need to take care of someone. And I am not only happy to be that someone, but I want to make sure that you are happy and have what you need."

"I am happy. I love you. We're together." He leaned into Charles's touch. "We're home."

"Mm. That's good enough for me. But if you think about it, and labels start to matter to you, I'm fine with that. I just wanted you to know that I see you. I understand you." Charles bent for a kiss. "And I love you."

"I love you too." And that was more than enough. More than.

"I'll let you finish." Mister Charlie smiled at him, then went back to his seat and his tea.

"I pulled out stew meat. I'm thinking beef and mushroom soup." He was craving a little bit. He liked to serve it over mashed potatoes sometimes.

"That sounds delicious. We can settle into the den and have a fire. My calendar is open, isn't it?"

"Yes, Sir. For a few days, actually." He winked.

"Oh, you're a wise cowboy." Mister Charlie grinned at him over his tea.

"Mhm." They were going to get to hang out for a bit, and he couldn't wait.

19

Charles hit the end-call button on his desk phone with a sigh. He was happy to be sitting on this nonprofit board; he had the time and the energy, but it required patience and tact, and he was just about out of that for the day.

He reached for his tea, surprised when he didn't find the mug on its warmer on his desk. Ryder usually snuck in with a mug for him when he was on the phone.

He chuckled at himself. He was so spoiled.

At least he knew as much. No tea on his desk was far from the end of the world. He picked up his cell and texted Ryder.

CHARLES

Could you please bring me a cup of tea when you have a moment?

He looked at that, finger hovering over the send button, then deleted it. He was capable of getting his own tea. He got up and headed for the kitchen.

"Leave me the fuck alone today, guys. My fucking head hurts, and I don't feel like talking in circles. Later?"

"But, Ry—"

"I said, not today, kiddo. Y'all live in Momma's house, so you live by her rules. And before you ask, no. No, you can't live here."

The twins, he assumed.

He snuck in and opened a cabinet to get a mug, then opened the tea drawer.

"I. Said. No." There was a sharp crack, and then a soft sigh. "Fuck."

He looked up, closed the drawer, and went to Ryder. He didn't want to interrupt so he just gently slid a hand over his cowboy's shoulders to let Ryder know he was there.

Ryder sighed, soft and low. "Hey. Do you need anything? I was... I had to deal with some sh-stuff."

"I heard. Family first, remember?" Charles kissed Ryder's temple. "I just came in for some tea."

"Oh, I'll get you some, no problem." Ryder stood up, foot tangling in the chair, and he went stumbling.

"Whoa." He caught Ryder easily. "Let me. Would you like some?"

"Oh God. I'm sorry. I'm so clumsy. How was your meeting? Do you want cookies?"

Nothing rattled Ryder the way his family could. They were good people, but somehow Ryder's siblings couldn't seem to make any decisions without him. "I don't need cookies, thank you." He made his way back to the tea drawer and pulled out a box.

He thought something calming, without caffeine. Something to soothe Ryder's nerves. "The meeting was fine, though I wish some people would get to the point faster."

He grabbed a second mug and used the InstaHot to fill

them. Supposedly that was cheating, but it was much faster than waiting for water to boil. "Do you want to tell me what's going on at home?"

"Just the boys. They're chomping at the bit to get out of the house, get to rodeoing." Ryder shook his head and sighed. "It's a mess."

"Hm." He pulled Ryder into his arms. "You don't have to hold the family together. They have the same mother you did, and you turned out okay."

"I know. I'm trying to make them understand, but they just don't."

"Would you have at their age? I'm no parent, but it seems to me that teenagers are all made of the same thing. Impatience."

"We were riding full-time on our eighteenth birthday. They still have nine months, and they have to finish high school." Ryder shook his head. "I wish—" He stopped and shrugged. "What a day."

"Tell me your wish." He pushed a mug of tea over to Ryder and the honey pot too.

"Thank you." Ryder sweetened his tea with a liberal splash of honey.

"You're welcome." But Ryder hadn't answered him. "Are you ignoring me or did you not hear the question?"

"I feel bad about telling. I feel like a shitty person."

He slid his fingers over Ryder's white hair. "The beautiful thing about an intimate relationship is you can say anything you want without judgment."

"I just wish they'd call Roper. Or that someone else would do it for a little while so I can focus on us."

He understood why Ryder felt that thought made him a bad person. "That's okay, you know. Old habits are hard to break. You're redefining yourself, and they're not ready for it.

Have you tried not answering the phone? Because that is an option. If you don't answer, maybe then they will actually call Roper."

"Maybe..." Ryder jumped as his phone rang again, and the hot tea spilled, landing in Ryder's lap. "Mother *fucker*!"

"*Boy*." The word just came out of his mouth like it was the most natural thing in the world, and he didn't question it. He took the mug and put it on the counter. "Sit. Don't answer it."

Ryder blinked at him.

Then he sat.

"Give me your phone." He held his hand out for it expectantly and didn't intend to have an argument.

Ryder's hand was shaking, but he handed it over, no question.

"Thank you. Now, please go upstairs and change into something dry, something softer—sweatpants perhaps— and wait for me in the bedroom. I'm going to clean up here, and then I'll join you." He wanted to give Ryder a moment without eyes on him, but only a moment, not long enough for him to spiral again.

"I'm sorry for spilling the tea. I can clean it..."

"I don't care about the tea. I care about you." He took a step closer and caught Ryder's chin in his fingers. "I care about you."

Was he wrong, or were there tears in Ryder's eyes? "I care about you too."

He didn't let himself go too deep into what the tears meant yet. He wanted to be comfortable; he wanted to hold Ryder in his arms and listen. "I know. And I love you for that. Go upstairs and change. I'll be right there. I promise." He stepped back so Ryder could get up.

"Yes, Sir." Ryder headed upstairs, rubbing the back of his neck on the way.

He sighed and looked at Ryder's phone, then set it on silent and placed it on the kitchen counter, leaving his own right beside it. It took him all of five minutes to put the mugs in the dishwasher and clean up the spilled tea, and then he was on his way up the stairs to Ryder.

To his...boy. Lover. Cowboy.

To the man who needed him right now.

That thought had him taking the final few steps two at a time. He stepped through the partially closed bedroom door and glanced around for Ryder.

Ryder had on a pair of sweatpants, a huge sweatshirt, and he had been staring out the window until he heard Charles, then he stood.

He kicked off his shoes and went right to Ryder, arms open. "Come here."

"Yes, Sir." Ryder burrowed into his embrace, arms wrapping around him.

"I've got you. Just let the noise go. It's just you and me now." He held Ryder tight, nose pressed against the top of Ryder's head. "You can say anything you like, ask for anything you need. It won't leave this room."

"I needed a hug. I have the worst headache."

He held on, absorbing Ryder's anxiety and returning all the calm strength he could muster. "Can I get you something? Tylenol? I was thinking we could lie down. Talk."

"I'd like to lie down with you. Please. If you're not too busy."

"I am never too busy for you. You're the most important person in my life. My phone is with yours downstairs, and it's going to stay there so we're not interrupted by anyone." He let Ryder go long enough to remove his dress pants and his jacket and pull on a pair of sweatpants so they'd both be comfortable.

"My so-formal man." Ryder beamed at him. "Don't forget your socks. Your feet get cold."

He snorted because that made him feel a thousand years old. "I think they'll be warm enough with you in my arms."

"I hope so. I hope you're always warm enough with me." Sweet cowboy poet.

"Let's put it to the test." He pulled Ryder to the bed and climbed on, reaching for the cozy blanket at the foot and pulling that up.

Ryder snuggled in, almost clinging to him. "I'm sorry. It's been a shit day."

"If all we had were good days, we wouldn't appreciate them. And I can't think of a single thing you've done for which you owe me, or anyone, an apology." He rubbed Ryder's back and took slow, deep breaths, hoping to encourage his cowboy to do the same.

Ryder kissed his jaw. "I want to be nothing but good, even though that's not reasonable."

"It's not reasonable; you're correct. You can't hold yourself to an impossible standard, or you'll be disappointed. Often. I certainly don't expect perfection, though I understand the desire." He smiled at Ryder's kisses and let himself just enjoy them.

"Yeah, I like being one of the good things in your life."

"You are. Even when you're having a bad day. Maybe especially then, because I get to remind you how wonderful you are." Charles ducked as Ryder lifted his head to kiss his chin. He caught Ryder's lips instead, taking a kiss of his own.

Ryder opened to him, loving him and letting him in.

"Mm. See? Wonderful."

"It is. You are." Ryder snuggled in closer, wrapping around him.

"How would you feel if I kept your phone for a little while?" Maybe that wasn't reasonable, but Ryder needed to break the habit of letting his family interrupt whenever they pleased. For his own sanity.

"How would you call me? How would I access your calendar? You need me to have access, lover."

"Well, I could buy you a laptop..." He tilted his head. "Or a private phone. Just one for you and me. Something that's only ours." He could feel Ryder tense up a little. "Certainly not forever. Just now and again when you need a break so they learn to function without you once in a while."

Ryder sighed softly. "I could... I could really think about it. I just need some breathing room."

"Let's try it. I'll add another line to my plan tomorrow. Uh—to our plan."

"Our plan." Ryder sighed and stroked his back. "What do you do for Thanksgiving and Christmas? Do you celebrate?"

He'd known they would be having this conversation soon. It was fall, the holidays were coming, and Ryder had family. "Tad hated Christmas. And most holidays. So..." They'd gone to parties in the city, but they'd never celebrated at home.

"Oh. What...what about you, though?" Ryder's hands stroked his belly, slow and sweet.

He shrugged, answering that question with a question because if wasn't sure what the answer was. "You're the one with family. What do you do?"

"We're big on holidays. I've spent a few not at home— riding in Hawaii, injured, what-have-you, but Roper's always been there."

"Where will Roper be for Thanksgiving? We can go there." That was a simple answer.

"Home with the folks, probably." Ryder rolled his eyes. "Honestly, I don't know. Let me ask. Later. That's all complicated, always. I want to introduce you to the family, but do you really want to meet them all at once?"

"I want you to have the holidays you want. If that's with them, then that's what I want to do. I don't have any family, but you do."

"Okay." Ryder seemed to tense. "I'll work it out."

Perhaps that wasn't the right idea. "Or we could go away."

"Where? Do people...go away for Thanksgiving? Is that even possible?"

"Sure. An all-inclusive resort somewhere snowy or a beach in Mexico. Anywhere we want." He dropped his voice to a whisper. "We're adults."

"I—Do you want to?" Ryder looked at him, eyes wide.

An all-inclusive resort with his lover sounded like the perfect Thanksgiving to him. "I think it sounds great. Do you?"

"I do. I mean, just you and me, no fights, no cooking, no washing up. Just us, together..."

"A snowy resort maybe. You and I basking in our food coma in front of a roaring fireplace." The more they talked about it the better it sounded. "Or the pool. I don't care. You pick."

Ryder's eyes lit up. "Oh, snow. Please. I would love that."

"I will find us a snowy Thanksgiving. We'll have turkey and a great view and a warm fire." They'd have to go north or west for snow. Buffalo, Denver, Jackson Hole—he would do some research.

"I can't believe this. I can't believe it's possible to just...do this. Celebrate somewhere else."

He laughed gently. "Ryder, we can do anything we want. It will be fun." It would be easy and relaxing, and it was nothing like what he and Tad used to do, which was perfect. This was something different, just for them. "We'll stay stateside for Thanksgiving since it's coming up soon, but maybe we'll go to Europe for Christmas. I've heard wonderful things about the Christmas markets in Germany. Berlin. Hamburg, I think. Dresden."

"I have a passport, and I know how to use it." Ryder rubbed their noses together. "I am a go-baby."

"Then we're going to go, cowboy." He could take Ryder anywhere. But right now, all he wanted to do was stay right here.

"Wow. I love the idea. You. Me. Together. Celebrating."

"I think we should start right now." He caught Ryder, hauling him up onto his chest. "Kiss me."

"Oh, yes Sir." Ryder framed his face, diving in to offer him a long, slow, lazy burning kiss.

He held on, pinning Ryder to his chest with one arm and returned the kiss, perfectly happy to go up in flames.

He could feel his lover—his boy—getting hard against him, Ryder's hips beginning to rock almost immediately.

"Feeling better?" Charles certainly was. He was warm and aroused, a little high on the idea that he had that effect on someone like Ryder. He tugged at Ryder's T-shirt, wiggling it over that silver-haired head.

"Yes, Sir. I like a little afternoon delight with you. It feels naughty."

"It does a little bit, doesn't it?" He rolled up, lifting Ryder with his hips. "Sweats off?"

"Mmhmm…" Ryder reached and eased his sweats down and off his needy cock.

He slid his hands up Ryder's sides, fingers gliding over muscle unlike anything he'd ever handled before.

"Feels good, lover. You have warm hands, I swear to God." Ryder wiggled in his hands.

"You have beautiful skin." It was smooth and darker than his. Ryder had a fair amount of scars though, some of them rather intense-looking. He'd never thought to ask about them, but perhaps he would later as pillow talk.

"No one's ever said that to me before…" Ryder stole another hard kiss. "Thank you."

"You're welcome. The truth comes easy around you." He pushed at the waistband of Ryder's sweats, and the elastic caught around his lover's cock, the hard flesh bouncing up and slapping against Ryder's flat belly. The fleeting cross-eyed look on the boy's face made him grin. "Terribly sorry."

"Uh-huh." Ryder's husky laugh made his smile wider. "You are so mean to my poor prick."

"No, I'm not. It's my favorite thing." He circled his fingers around it. "I'll make it feel better."

"Yes, Sir. I believe you will." Ryder pushed right into his touch.

He lifted a foot and pushed Ryder's sweats all the way down and Ryder wiggled them over his feet, which would have been cute except that it rocked their hips together in a way that made him groan.

He'd wanted Tad every day they were together. He didn't always get what he wanted. Tad had always been flirty but not always as sexual as he was. He didn't know what he'd do if Ryder didn't want as much as he did, since he could hardly keep his hands off the boy.

It didn't seem to be an issue. Ryder was eager for him,

watched him with hunger, and let him know it. He reached down and pulled one of Ryder's knees up so the cowboy was straddling his hips, then leaned up for another kiss.

Ryder's core strength stunned him, as he leaned down without using Charles's hands to hold him up.

"You're incredible," he whispered against Ryder's lips before they kissed. Their connection was always strong, often hungry, and this was no exception.

When their lips parted, Ryder moaned. "I'm all yours. Every inch."

"I want you. All of that." He reached for the lube, which was never hard for him to find, and poured the cool liquid on his fingers. "Scooch up so I can reach you." His voice was so gravelly it sounded like he was half wild animal.

Ryder beamed at him, kneeling up tall, offering him that hard, tight little body, cock bobbing like a flagpole.

He tucked his hand under those heavy balls and found Ryder's hot little hole waiting for him. He circled the boy's cock with his other hand and worked it slowly, just enough to give Ryder too much to think about.

Ryder's lips parted, and his head fell back, exposing the long column of his throat.

"Beautiful." He pushed his slippery fingers inside his boy and worked them around, making sure Ryder was going to be ready to ride.

Ryder moved unlike anyone he'd ever seen, rocking and sliding, taking his fingers in, again and again. Watching was making him ache, and he didn't want to wait.

He withdrew his fingers, and the next time Ryder rocked, he replaced them with his prick.

Ryder arched, the sweetest long groan filling the air as a dark flush climbed his belly. "Oh, damn... You're everywhere."

He swallowed, trying to find his voice. "You feel like heaven."

"I do." Ryder settled on him, taking him to the root.

He groaned and rested his hands on Ryder's thighs as his cowboy started to move, his gaze roaming over every muscle, every bit of Ryder's skin.

"Love how you fill me up. Need you."

"I'm right here. You can have everything you need."

Ryder smiled at him, hands dragging up and down his body, teasing both of them.

"A month ago, you'd have rushed this, you know." He winked at Ryder, teasing right back.

"A month ago, I was convinced I had to. This is better."

"So much better." Ryder did...something—moved in some way that sent fire up his spine and made it hard to get a deep breath. "So good."

"Uh-huh. Don't stop. Please. I'm aching."

Charles had no intention of stopping. He worked Ryder's cock through his hand and they rocked together, giving him everything he needed to spiral higher.

Every stroke made Ryder's eyes cross, and that sweet ass clenched around him.

He watched Ryder's face. It was so expressive, and he loved to see Ryder's pleasure and desire. He also loved to see Ryder shoot, and he worked that pretty cock, teasing his thumb across the swollen head over and over.

"M-mister Charlie. Love. So fucking close." Ryder's eyes rolled back in his head.

He knew. He knew what every grimace meant, every twitch of that sweet body around his cock. Ryder knew what he liked too, and he liked it when his cowboy came first. "Beautiful boy."

"Yours." Ryder stared into him, his eyes so intense, so very hungry for him.

He stared right back, not shying away from the intimacy at all. He and Ryder shared every truth now, including this one. Especially this one. "Mine. Come for me, beautiful cowboy."

"Yes, Sir. Anything for you." Ryder moaned, hot seed pouring over his fingers.

He grunted as Ryder's body vibrated around his cock. Jesus, he fucking loved that. He rolled up, fingers holding on to Ryder's hips and rocked under his boy, sweet friction and heat pushing him right to the edge. He fought for a second to hold himself there because it felt so damn good, but it was a losing battle and just a couple of hard thrusts later, he was lost, shooting hard and diving off that cliff after his boy.

Ryder let him ride his pleasure out, moving in the tiniest hip rolls to keep the aftershocks going. His cowboy was determined to drive him out of his mind.

He shivered, letting Ryder send him wherever the boy wanted to. "I can't resist you. It's terrible and wonderful."

"You don't have to." Ryder rested against him. "I didn't come here to fall in love, but I did."

"I don't know. Perhaps that is precisely why you came here. It was just what we both needed, at just the right moment, which is hard to consider complete happenstance." His mother used to tell him that everything happened for a reason.

"Yes. I like to believe this means something. You mean a lot to me." Ryder stroked his chest, the touch languid.

He caught those fingers and kissed them. "Ryder, you are the most important person in my life. When you have something you're dealing with, I'm here to lean on, to give advice if you want it or just listen if you don't. You're never, ever a burden, so please, come to me when you're overwhelmed, and we'll work through it. Just...give it to me. I'm here for you."

"Yeah? That sounds...wonderful and hard at the same time." Ryder chewed on his bottom lip. "I'm so used to having Roper all the time, but—I don't know, Mister Charlie. I feel... I don't know. Maybe I should just shut up."

He hugged Ryder closer and chuckled. "Didn't I just tell you to talk more?"

"Yes, Sir. You sure did. I love this—it feels special, to be in bed in the daylight, you know?"

"Decadent. A little naughty? I can't think of anything I'd rather be doing."

Ryder beamed at him. "Me either. God knows, this is the second most fun I've had in this bed today."

He laughed loud. Possibly the loudest he ever had in bed. "Me too. Maybe we will make tonight our third."

"God, I hope so, lover. I sure do hope so."

20

———

"You can't just not come home for Thanksgiving! Son, you will not just...leave!"

Ryder put his phone on mute and put it on the bed to keep packing for their trip.

"Ryder? Are you hearing me? Hello?"

"Oh, he hears you." Mister Charlie rolled his eyes and set their coats on the bed as well.

"I do. She's really pissed." Ryder shook his head and sighed. "Roper is heading to Hawaii."

"Did he decide that after you told him you weren't going home?"

"Ryder? Are you still there?" His uncle was on the phone now.

"He did. He's a coward."

"Goddamn it, Ryder!"

Ryder jumped, his heart hiccupping, and he reached for his phone, automatically.

"No." His hand landed on top of Charles's hand. Charles picked up the phone and hung up the call. "I'm turning it off, and we're leaving it here."

He searched Charles's eyes. "It's okay? I don't want to hurt them, but I'm so excited."

"They don't seem to care if they hurt you, but I do. I won't allow anyone to speak to you that way. That's not love. The phone stays here, you can bring your other one. They don't deserve to be a part of our holiday." Mister Charlie shut it off just like he said he would and set it on the dresser. "Done."

"I—Yes, Sir." He took a deep, deep breath, letting it stretch his lungs, then he blew it out. "Do we need anything else?"

"Yes, I need to know if you're all right." Mister Charlie stepped closer and rested a hand on his bicep.

"It's hard, huh? But I'm tickled as all get out to go on this trip with you. I really am." Ryder hadn't even done anything this...utterly selfish and wonderful, ever.

"You've made a choice to finally do something for yourself, and they're not happy about it and are trying to make you feel like it's a mistake." Mister Charlie pressed a hand to his chest. "You'd know if it was a mistake. You'd feel it, here."

"I hate that they hurt, but I don't regret going," he admitted.

"I am very much looking forward to it as well. We have an amazing suite; you're going to love it. At least, I hope you will love it." Mister Charlie bent and kissed his cheek. "Finish up. The car will be here soon."

"Yes, Sir. Are you sure we'll have enough to do?" he teased. They could spend hours and hours just talking, playing cards. They enjoyed each other's company.

"I'm sure we'll manage. After all, one day we'll spend eating our own body weight in turkey, and the next we'll be in bed all day sleeping it off. We could always try to break our record."

"Are you talking about lazing in bed records or multiple orgasm records?" It was an important distinction.

"Why not both? We could make them one and the same. The bedroom has a fireplace and a Jacuzzi tub, and room service is included so, in theory, we wouldn't have to go anywhere at all."

"Ooh...snow. Fire. Bubbles. I might just pop one off now..."

Mister Charlie laughed. "The car will be here any second, but I'm happy to watch if you can hurry..."

He cracked up, wrapping his arms around his lover. "Thank you, Mister Charlie. For being you."

He got a big bear hug in return. "Mhm. You too, my love." Charles's phone rang, and he could feel it vibrate against his hip. "That's the car, I bet."

"We're going to go play!" He might have bounced. "I'll grab the bags."

Mister Charlie answered the phone while he wrestled their bags downstairs. "We're on our way. Yes, plenty of time. Oh, Ryder is on his way with our luggage. I'm sure he'd appreciate the help. Thank you."

He grabbed his coat and started moving bags to the landing. It was almost like getting ready to ride.

He glanced at his phone. "Sorry, Momma. I needed to do this, for me."

Mister Charlie picked up a suitcase and carried it down the stairs. "We have about a three-hour drive, so we can look at the brochure on the way and make some plans if you want to."

"Sounds perfect." He smiled, nodded. "Happy Thanksgiving, Sir."

Charles stopped moving and smiled at him. "Happy Thanksgiving, Ryder. I'm so glad we're doing this."

"I am too. I love you, Sir. Let's go play."

They were out the door and getting comfy in the car in no time, and Charles had an arm around him as they left the lake house behind.

He didn't even start sitting apart from Charles. No, he snuggled right into his lover's side. He knew how his man was on long car rides. Charles would be dozing before too long.

"What are you looking forward to the most, lover?" He was eager to see the snow, to relax, and not deal with fighting and politics.

"Letting you be as pampered as I usually am. You won't have to cook, clean, make a bed...nothing."

"I'll just get to love on you. It sounds like heaven." Nothing to do but be...a couple.

"Mhm. Something to celebrate and be thankful for. Have you ever been skiing?"

"I have, sort of. I've done the Cowboy Downhill in Steamboat Springs a few years. I only fell eighty times..."

"This sounds like one of those things I need to look up on YouTube." Mister Charlie liked to tease him.

"Totally. Look up rodeo twins crash and burn on the slopes." He cracked up.

Charles pulled out his phone and grinned at him. "Oh, did you mean later? You probably meant later."

He grabbed Charles's phone and found the video. He wasn't ashamed; he thought it was hilarious. He'd rolled down the damn slope.

"Oh, my goodness. Oh. Ouch." Charles grinned, then chuckled, then laughed out loud.

"I know. We were snowballs. It was great." They had had a ball goofing off.

"That looks like fun. Painful, but fun." Charles put his phone away. "When is he coming to visit? I think he should come to New York. I wouldn't mind if you'd like him to join us for Christmas. Europe can wait."

"That would be fun. Roper would love that. He's going to be in almost as much trouble as I am." Ryder was the 'good' one. Roper always got in more trouble.

Charles snorted. "I will be even more unpopular with your mother than I already am. You should feel free to make whatever invitation you would like. Just let me know what the plans are."

"I'll talk to him after our vacation. I'm officially out of pocket until next week."

"Mm. Yes. You're officially in my pocket until then."

"Oooh... I like your pocket, my love." He liked it a lot.

"Me too." Charles hunkered down a little in his seat and closed his eyes. "Me too."

He leaned against Mister Charlie's shoulder, grabbed his book, and settled in. He had nothing to worry about but his man.

CHARLES WOKE up when the car stopped moving. He'd been dozing—well, who was he kidding, he'd fallen asleep—and the whole trip had gone by quickly.

He often felt a little car sick on long drives, but he'd never admit to that. It seemed better to just doze off and let Ryder think he was a fuddy-duddy.

He was a bit of a fuddy-duddy anyway.

He stretched and sat up, smiling at Ryder, who was so

excited he could almost feel his lover vibrating from across the back seat.

Ryder had devoured his book, and he was zipping through the final chapters.

"This resort comes highly recommended." It had a high price tag, but it was off the beaten path, and they would be treated like kings.

"Does it?" Ryder grinned at him. "It's gorgeous. Just like a storybook. I approve."

Ryder was right, it did look like a storybook. A-frame snow-covered roofs, warm light in the windows, running cedar, and twinkling white lights made it feel festive too. He slid out of the car and held a hand out for Ryder.

Ryder took his hand and stood, holding on. "Do I need to grab the suitcases?"

"The only thing you need to grab is me." He put an arm over Ryder's shoulders and pulled him hip-to-hip.

They climbed up the wide front steps, shivering a little until they got through the front doors to the lobby where it was warm and smelled like a wood fire.

"Welcome." A middle-aged woman stood behind the shining wood counter. "Mr. Martin, you made exceptional time."

"I confess I dozed off so it was a very quick trip for me." He glanced at her nametag. "Ah, Valerie. You're the one I spoke with on the phone. This is my partner, Ryder Vales."

"Mr. Vales, pleased. We're so glad to have you as our guests. I have all of your room information and keys here. You have a lovely suite, and we're at your service."

He reached for the keys. "Thank you. Two questions, where is dinner, and could we have hot cocoa and marshmallows delivered to the room please?"

Valerie smiled warmly. "Dinner is at seven, and you'll

have an assigned table for the duration of your stay. It has a lovely view. I think you'll like it. And cocoa will be up shortly."

"Perfect. Thank you very much." He watched as their luggage made its way down the hall.

Ryder held one hand out to shake. "It's been grand to meet you. Thank you for the warm welcome."

Ryder might have thought his mother was a handful, but she did something right raising her boy. He was a pleasure to take anywhere.

Valerie's smile was surprised and pleased. She shook his hand. "Very nice to meet you, too. If you want anything special while you're here, just give me a call."

"Thank you, ma'am. I appreciate it." Then Ryder was at his side, arm twining with his. "Cocoa, huh? How fancy."

"Fun. Less fancy, more fun." He tucked that arm close as they followed their luggage into the elevator. "Do you know how kind you are? Everyone tells me so, everywhere I go."

"Am I? I just treat folks like I'd want to be treated, but that's nice to hear."

"That makes you special. Not everyone does that. I appreciate it." He was surprised at the size of the place as they got off the elevator. It had looked much smaller from downstairs, but up here there were sitting areas, big windows, and the hallways were nice and wide. Their room was far enough down the hall to be free from elevator noise, and the bellhop let them in.

It was charming and lush, with Christmas lights delicately framing the windows. The fireplace was blazing, and the bed was huge and covered in a white duvet. There was a sitting area in front of the fire, and the whole thing screamed, "relax".

He sank into the comfy couch in front of the fireplace

and started it with a remote control. "I know you; you'll want to unpack right away, so I'll just sit here and keep an ear out for our cocoa, shall I?" He was only half teasing. Ryder did like to make everywhere they stayed together feel like home.

"Sounds perfect to me. I want to get our shirts hung up. I hate wrinkled shirts." Ryder leaned down and kissed him, soft and slow.

"Mmm." Charles didn't care about wrinkles, or much of anything else at the moment. Just that Ryder was happy, and he seemed to be. He had luggage to deal with and an empty closet to fill and, as lazy as it made Charles look not to help, Ryder needed that. He needed to feel useful. He enjoyed doing while Charles sat and relaxed.

And Charles had dealt with the angry family, giving Ryder the headspace he needed.

Headspace was something he was learning about from River and Victor. They had a group text going, and he used it frequently. Charles was trying to give Ryder what he needed without using the customary lifestyle words that their friends—and even Roper—used. Ryder didn't like them; they made him anxious. They added pressure somehow, or perhaps even frightened Ryder. He wasn't sure.

Whatever it was, he was respectful. Labels didn't matter. Health and happiness mattered. Love mattered.

Ryder mattered.

There was a knock at the door. That had to be the cocoa. He slid off the couch to answer it.

"Do you want to explore the place a little before dinner?"

"That sounds like fun. It's bigger than it seems, isn't it?" Ryder came in wearing a huge sweater. "Ooh, hot chocolate!"

"Be careful, it *is* hot." The kid from room service gave them a wink as he set the tray down on the coffee table. "We make it from scratch with milk, and we even make our own marshmallows. You're going to love it."

He reached for his wallet as the kid started to leave.

"No tips but thank you. You paid for them in your service fee."

"All right." He'd tip a lump sum the day they left. "Thank you for the drinks."

"You're welcome. Have a nice evening."

Charles closed the door after the kid. "No tips. Quite a place. I hope I didn't insult him."

"I bet it's fine. He'll get his part from the resort fees or what-have-you."

His lover was very hotel literate, wasn't he?

"You've done your research? Or have you just stayed in that many hotels?" He dropped a couple of the homemade marshmallows into each mug and brought one to Ryder.

"I've lived all my adult life in hotels, Sir. Literally, I've never had a home of my own. We were either in hotels or at home at the folks'."

"Right, of course. I wasn't thinking. You spent all your time on the road. But it seems like having a home suits you." He sniffed his cocoa and hummed, then took a tiny sip, testing how hot it was. "Oh. Yum."

"Is it amazing?" Ryder took a sip and groaned. "It is, and I love having a place. It suits me, having a solid spot, a routine. I like it."

He nodded because he knew. "I like that you're such a good cook, and you spoil me." He took another sip, letting the rich chocolate slide over his tongue. This was a good idea.

"I like that you are the best to chat with and read with and…" Ryder blushed and grinned. "Snuggle with."

"Mm. I like how you can't sit still when we snuggle." He waggled his eyebrows at Ryder.

"Well… I am a healthy gay man with the hottest thing ever doing the snuggling."

"Mhm. Put that thought away, healthy gay man. I'm making you wait until after dinner. I want to go explore after we have our cocoa." He liked making Ryder wait. The little buzz helped the cowboy relax. He liked making himself wait too; it was good for him, to keep Ryder in mind, but not always in bed.

"Sounds good. I'm curious to see everything. It's… friendly, right? Like for men like us?"

As if he would take Ryder somewhere not friendly. "Men like us—you mean gay couples? It's friendly. It's not exclusively for men, but it's openly welcoming. And it's not a very big place; it's not like one of those enormous resorts right? So we'll see a lot of the same people around."

"Cool. I wouldn't want you to be uncomfortable at all." Ryder watched out for him so well.

And in return it was his job—his pleasure—to look after Ryder. "I wouldn't want you to be either, love. This is our holiday."

"Yes." Oh, didn't Charles love that sweet, happy little grin.

He put his mug down. It was sweet and delicious, but very rich. "I think that's enough of that for me. I don't want to ruin dinner."

"It's super sweet. I would want it in coffee, I think. It would be like a fancy drink."

"Oh, a mocha. That sounds good. We'll try that tomorrow afternoon while we're lounging in front of the fireplace." He stood and offered Ryder a hand. "Are you done with unpacking? Ready to go look around?"

"I am, and I am!" Ryder took his hand with a grin. "Let's go explore."

"I have been told there is a heated outdoor swimming pool, which I think we should try out at some point. We can snowshoe also. Have you ever been snowshoeing?"

"I haven't, but I love to swim. It's one of my favorite exercises."

How did he not know that? "I was thinking more along the float and drink wine lines than exercise, but I am happy to watch you swim."

There was plenty of room at the lake house for a pool...

"Oh, I can swim and float and... I've never floated with wine."

"I don't believe I have either, but it sounds lovely, doesn't it?" He put an arm around Ryder as they left the room. It was dark, so it was hard to see out the windows, but he could tell by the frost and the snow settled on the sills that they were in for a treat in the morning.

"It so does." Ryder was wide-eyed. "I love to imagine the inner workings of hotels, don't you? It's got to be a little like an airport."

"There is most certainly all manner of prep work and organization going on behind the scenes, but all we see is cocoa and warm fires."

"Right? All the people who have to work for us to have an amazing time?" Ryder's eyes crinkled at the edges. "So cool."

"Could be a good career for you. If you needed a career, which you don't." He chuckled. "You're busy. And taken."

"I am. And I am, balls to bones." Ryder gave him a grin.

"So crude, my cowboy lover." He winked at Ryder. "I think I see a Christmas tree."

"Oh, are you a multi-colored light person or a designer tree type?"

"Hm. I like both. I appreciate the themed trees that someone has obviously put a great deal of thought into, but I also enjoy the family-type tree with colored lights and silly ornaments collected over the years." He shrugged. "I've never had a tree as an adult, so I think I'd be happy with anything."

"Well, I think we should start with one ornament, and see what happens, what calls to us, then."

"I do love how you think. I love that you're thinking about beginnings and new traditions. We should see if they have something in the gift shop we can take home with us." He led Ryder into a big open room with couches and several central fireplaces. It had a warm and cozy feel to it despite its size.

"Oh, that would be perfect." Ryder moved toward the fire, warming his hands.

He slid behind Ryder, ghosting a hand over that tight ass, then wandered over to the enormous Christmas tree, It was real, and it smelled amazing.

The tree was a riot of colors—hung with huge to tiny balls that reflected all the lights. It was absolutely breathtaking.

Perhaps it was selfish of him, but he didn't regret taking Ryder away from his family for the holidays. This feeling, and the relaxed look on Ryder's face, was enough to convince him it had been the right move. They were basking in each other, and that was how it should be.

Ryder appeared behind him, arms wrapping around his waist. "Mmm...you smell good, Sir."

"How is the fire? I was going to see for myself, but the tree called to me."

"It's so pretty, isn't it? I love the colors." Ryder held him until someone came into the big lobby.

"Where'd you go?" He reached back and put an arm around Ryder's shoulders. Friendly meant they were allowed to be a couple near the Christmas tree and anywhere else they pleased. "Got you."

Ryder blinked a second, then eased right in, relaxing into him.

"Better, right? We're okay here."

As far as he was concerned, they were okay everywhere.

21

Ryder floated in their Jacuzzi tub, a glass of wine in hand, just about as happy as a pig in shit.

They'd Thanksgiving'd until they were both fixin' to explode. Then they'd gone to a football party and laughed their asses off.

Now it was Friday night, and he was feeling lazy and a touch tipsy.

"Thank you for thinking about us, gentlemen; we are having a lovely time. Yes, we'll be in town for Christmas. Same to you. Mhm. Bye bye." Charles had been wandering the room in a robe that was tied so loosely it was basically useless and a glass of wine in one hand. He set the phone down on the nightstand. "River and Kayce and Vincent all say hello. They wanted to say we were missed at the club's Thanksgiving dinner and invited us to Christmas. I didn't make any promises."

The robe dropped to the floor, and Charles stepped into the tub with him. "Oh. Nice."

"Right? Hot bubbles. Roper's going to come for

Christmas. You know he is." Ryder wasn't going to bother to even doubt.

No way was Roper braving Momma without him.

"I'm sure he'll be welcome to join us at the club, if that's what we decide we want to do. And you know he's welcome with us in any case." Charles refilled their glasses, then eased into the water with a sigh.

"Mmhmm." He floated right over, settling in Charles's lap.

"Much easier to drink in the tub than the pool." Charles curled an arm around him so he didn't float away.

"Uh-huh. Hey, beautiful." He lifted his face for a kiss. "Having the best time."

He'd never had such a low-stress turkey day.

He got his kiss. Charles tasted like white wine and fresh fruit. "You make me want to drop everything and just travel with you forever. Make love in every tourist destination and back road B and B everywhere."

"Mmm...that is an amazing goal. We'd miss home, eventually. You would miss my pot pie." He winked to show he was teasing and stole another kiss.

Charles chuckled against his lips. "And your cookies. My God, would I miss those oatmeal whatevertheyare's."

"Mmm...oatmeal scotchies for the win, right?" He needed to make a batch when they got home, along with some shortbread.

"Scotchies! Yes, those would be very much missed. And I am somewhat attached to the lake house." Charles winked. Ryder had made no secret that it was his favorite place too.

Charles set his glass aside. "We have to go home tomorrow, but we don't have to be in the city for a week or so, correct? So we can try to hold on to some of this marvelous vacation energy for a little longer."

"Vacation energy... I like that. Low key. Less phone. More one on one." Ryder was in. He had stopped thinking about his phone, about stress. It was amazing.

His head had stopped hurting.

"More one on one." Charles kissed him again, fingers sliding up his thigh.

His cock jerked, loving that touch. "Mmhmm...more exploring?"

"I believe so, yes." Charles cupped his balls, giving them a gentle tug.

His lips parted and his hips rocked, back and forth, a moan escaping him.

"I was thinking we could have dinner in the room tonight, unless your heart is set on the dining room again." Charles teased him with gentle fingers.

"Rooms are good..." He needed to focus...but how could he between wine and Mister Charlie?

"I thought so. I'm going to have dessert first though." Mister Charlie kissed him, and those gentle fingers wrapped around his prick, gliding slowly from root to tip.

"Dessert?" He arched, showing off a little, licking his lips.

"Mhm. You." Mister Charlie was watching, enjoying his show. "I've never made love in a hot tub before. Have you?"

He shook his head. "Not yet, love."

But he was ready to try, hell yes.

"Well, it's not the best idea from what I understand, but I have another idea, shall we try it?"

"I want to. Know. Try. The whole thing."

Charles chuckled, fingers curling tighter around him and stroking in earnest. "You sound distracted."

"Uh-huh." He was distracted. He was dizzy with wine and love.

"Every time I touch you I wonder why I waste my time doing anything else."

Oh, that made him soar, made him dive into another, harder, kiss.

Charles hummed and returned his kiss with such heat it was a wonder they didn't both turn to ashes.

He held Charles close, tilting his head and feeding off all that need.

Charles groaned and turned him so he was straddling those strong hips, then wrapped a big hand around both of their pricks, squeezing them together. "Need you."

"I'm yours. However you need me. Whenever you need me." It was a vow, from every ounce of him.

"Mine. My boy. My own." Charles worked their cocks together in long strokes.

"Uhn. Uh-huh. Uh-huh... Promise to God..." He was right there.

"Promise you—" Charles made that gorgeous, deep-throated sound he always did when he was about to shoot, then arched under him as that hand sped up.

"Love!" His balls drew up and that was that. He shot so hard his bones rattled.

"Yes—love." Charles held them together as their cocks jerked and rolled. They rode the aftershocks for a long time, before they collapsed together.

He leaned back and took Ryder's face in his hands. "I love you, Ryder. I haven't had an opportunity to say it the way I want to yet, but I do want to. I want you to hear it. I love you."

Ryder held his gaze, kissed him, long and slow. "Love you, Mister Charlie."

"I fucking love it here!" Roper grabbed Ryder as soon as he came out of the city apartment to let his twin in. "How could you ever leave?"

"The lake house is magic?" And he loved Charles, not where they were. "I'm so glad you're here. Merry almost Christmas!"

"Same to you!" Roper hauled two huge suitcases in, handing him one.

"Damn, Bubba, you got a body in here?"

"Christmas from the folks. All wrapped and everything."

Charles was waiting in the foyer and smiled as they hauled the suitcases inside. "Staying a few days, Roper? Ryder, you better show your brother his room before one of you hurts yourself."

"Yes, Sir."

"Hey, Charles! Merry Christmas! I brought presents for under the tree."

"Come on, butthead." He led Roper to the guest room. "Here you go."

"Nice!"

"Isn't it? I'm going to make it a little more homey, but it's still nice."

Roper parked one suitcase at the foot of the bed and took the other from him to do the same. "I can't believe I'm in New York. For Christmas."

"I'm tickled as shit, Bubba. I have missed your face." He took a hard hug, and they breathed together, nice and slow.

"Ditto. I'm glad to be here. It was time to see your place." Roper shrugged out of his coat. "Are you good? You look good. Charles is taking good care of you?"

"He's amazing. I'm happy. We spend a lot of time just... hanging out." And it was perfect. They talked, they played cards, they made love, they took walks.

"Ugh. Love. Gross." Roper squeezed his shoulders. "Damn good to see your stupid face."

"Good to see your ugly one. Jackass." They laughed together, both cracking up.

Roper took a breath. "I do need a break though. This is good. This is real good."

"I'm glad." It was tough, riding alone. Ryder knew it. He knew Roper's heart had to hurt.

Roper shook that off quickly. "Y'all got eggnog? I'll settle for a beer but..."

"It's homemade and everything. We bought it from this space in the grower's market."

"Yeah? For real? Let's go pour some." Roper followed him back toward the kitchen. "You got cookies too?"

"You know it."

There was a low chuckle from the living room, and his plate of snickerdoodles was missing from the kitchen counter.

"Oh, someone is celebrating already." He grinned. "Do you need a glass of eggnog, Mister Charlie?"

"That would be lovely, thank you. Come sit, Roper. Ryder will take care of things for us."

"Yeah? Okay. Okay, sure." Roper winked at him, teasing him, but he did like things a certain way, so he got the eggnog, topped it with nutmeg, and took it into the front room.

"How was your flight?" Charles held a half-eaten cookie in one hand. "I trust Alan took care of you on the ride from the airport?"

"It was great, and I have to say, he's a sweetheart. He knew all the hot spots, and he told me to insist on seeing Christmas windows."

"Everyone likes him. I'm very lucky to have him in my employ. We'll be tourists for a day or two for sure; if you haven't been to New York at Christmastime before, there is plenty to see." Charles took a cop of eggnog off his tray. "Thank you, love."

"Yes, Sir." He put the tray down and sat, offering Roper a glass. "I'm glad you're here to share the holidays, man. For real."

"I jumped on the invitation. I've been looking forward to spending Christmas with you." Roper looked at Mister Charlie. "And Charles, of course."

"Oh, I'm not fooled." Charles grinned. "I know why you're here."

"I'm here for my family, and you're part of that now." Roper winked. "Poor guy."

"Woe is me. If it means I get cookies and eggnog you are welcome any time." Charles smiled at Roper, then turned and winked at him. "We've been looking forward to having you. Please make yourself at home."

"Thank you. So this is home?"

Ryder chuckled. "Home is the lake house. This is the apartment."

Charles shrugged. "Ryder makes everywhere we go home."

Ryder's entire soul just melted, and he couldn't stop smiling.

Roper shook his head. "Damn, y'all. You're so sweet it makes my teeth hurt."

"You just like spicy, Bubba. Leave us to our sweet."

Roper nodded. "Hey, who am I to judge? Happy is happy. And it's Christmas."

"Yes. It is. And we're going to have one hell of a great vacation!" Ryder was so tickled. His lover, his twin, New York City.

Charles nodded. "We have dinner plans tonight, one of Ryder's favorites, and I think he wanted your assistance with decorating the tree. Tomorrow we'll take you to a men's club that a couple of my friends belong to. I'm sure Ryder has told you about the place."

"Yeah. Yes, Sir. I—I'm looking forward to that..." Roper licked his lips.

"No doubt you are." Charles sounded amused and hid a grin behind a sip of eggnog.

Ryder didn't want to think about that. At all.

He would just focus on Mister Charlie.

Charles didn't shy away at all. "I've been asked whether you're interested in being set up, or if you'd prefer to mingle and meet people?"

"From what my brother says, I'm better off getting introduced around, right? I don't want to waste time."

"Wise. I'll get you in touch with someone tomorrow so you can discuss what you need. They're quite welcoming to

—" Charles looked thoughtful, like he was choosing his words carefully. "Newcomers."

"They were amazing to me. So kind." Ryder had been welcomed with open arms, in fact.

"They are kind. That's an excellent assessment. It's a good place. I've been visiting with friends there for a few years. Not often, but enough that I know my way around now."

"Well, I know how to be on my very best behavior." Roper beamed at him.

"Good to know, but I think anyone there would tell you to just be yourself."

Roper's grin just went wider, and Ryder knew that look meant naughtiness.

Charles shook his head, smiling indulgently at Roper. "I picked the right twin."

"I hope so. I'd be lost if you decided you liked his ugly mug instead." In fact, he'd be devastated, but he knew that Charles loved him for him.

Charles laughed, bright and happy. "I hate to break it to you, Ryder, but he has the same *mug* that you do. It's a handsome mug. But I look deeper."

"Hey! I'm deep!" Roper winked at him, and they both cracked up, Ryder leaning into his lover.

Mister Charlie put an arm around his shoulders. He loved how Charles showed real interest in his brother. "You must be relieved to have a break."

"I am. It's harder than you'd think, going it alone." Roper shrugged, so unhappy. "I'm used to having Ry."

"I understand. I wouldn't want to do without him now either. Is it hard enough that you don't want to do it?"

"It's just not fun anymore. Why do it, if it's no fun?" Roper shrugged. "We're not getting rich, right?"

"Agreed. It's much too dangerous a sport to do for no good reason." Mister Charlie glanced at him, then back at Roper. "Are you saying you're retiring?"

"I don't know what I'm saying. It's Christmas. I'm not saying anything, right, Ry?"

"Totally."

"Got it. You're saying you need to put your feet up and sip your eggnog." Mister Charlie nodded.

"Exactly. I want to not think and enjoy y'all." Roper caught his gaze. "If I'd wanted to stress, I'd have stayed at the house, right?"

"You make a solid point. So, you haven't been here at Christmastime, right? Ryder and I put together a little tour for you. Well, two actually. One is a daytime tour, and the other is at night."

Ryder nodded, and he couldn't stop grinning. "You're going to love it. It'll make you smile."

"You know what I like, huh?" Roper winked at him, and Ryder felt a little like he was missing a joke.

Mister Charlie let it go and tucked him closer. "The eggnog is excellent, isn't it?"

"Amazing. It's one of my favorite parts of holiday food." He was about as happy as he could be.

Mister Charlie reached for another cookie but stopped himself. "How are you feeling, Roper? Do you need a rest after your flight? Or are you ready to see the city?"

"I'd like to just have a nap, if you don't mind. I want to go out tonight. I'll buy y'all supper."

"Of course. Please relax, have a nap. We want you to enjoy your vacation. Ryder and I are fond of naps."

Ryder's cheeks went red hot. "We...we so are."

Naked naps. With orgasms.

Charles didn't blush, he just smiled. "Ryder, why don't

you go help your brother settle in, show him where the towels are and such."

"Of course, Sir." He kissed Charles's cheek. "Come on, Bubba. I'll give you the nickel tour and let you breathe a little."

Roper followed him, then grabbed him, holding him tight for a long minute. "Love you."

"Ditto, cabbagehead." Ryder hugged Roper until he backed away. "Good nap."

"You know it." Roper gave him a nod and a smile that didn't seem as convincing as it should have been, then closed the guest room door quietly.

Ryder headed straight for Charles. He needed his lover. Right now.

He needed a hug; he needed direction. He needed Charles.

23

Charles didn't want a nap, but Ryder had certainly needed his company, so they'd been sitting by the fireplace reading for a while. Or more accurately, he'd been reading, and Ryder had been holding a book in his lap and sighing every so often. Charles had tea now, because the eggnog was delicious but very rich, and he picked it up to sip it, glancing at his lover as he set it down.

"Something is on your mind?" He had a fairly good idea of what it was, but when it came to Roper, words never came easily to Ryder. His boy was always worried about telling secrets or hurting his twin's feelings. "I'm right here."

"He seems unhappy. It feels wrong to be so happy when he's not. I have guilt."

He was right; he did know what was going on. "The two of you look alike, finish each other's sentences, but his path isn't your path. You can be happy to see him, happy to have him here. You can make him happy he decided to come, but you can't make him happy in life. He has to figure that out."

"I know. I do, but—I want him to be happy." Ryder held his hand.

"Because you love him. Of course you do." He had to wonder about Roper and what it would actually take to make him happy. If he was understanding correctly, whether Ryder wanted to admit it or not, Roper needed a very specific sort of relationship that seemed an unlikely find on the bull riding circuit. It was possible that Roper might find what he needed here in New York, however. "Maybe he'll like New York. He'd be welcome to stay."

Short term. He didn't think he wanted to live with Roper indefinitely. He honestly wasn't sure Ryder would either.

"For a little while, yes." Ryder winked at him, playing with him. "I love our lives."

"For a little while. Yes." He nuzzled Ryder's hair. "He'll be okay. Whatever he's going through will work itself out one way or another, and you're here for him, with him, in the meantime. That's what family is for. No guilt."

"No guilt it is. God, I love you. I'm so glad we're together."

"I am very glad." Charles shifted so he could look Ryder in the eye. "And whoever your brother needs to be happy is what it is. It's not for us to judge."

Ryder's head tilted. "What are you telling me, Sir?"

"That when we're at the club, you have to let him be himself."

"I do. I think I do." Ryder tilted his head. "Don't I?"

"Hm. I believe you want to, but you often look uncomfortable, and you're good at changing the subject." If he could feel Ryder's discomfort, surely Roper did too.

Ryder sighed softly. "He's just very...sexual."

That was an interesting observation, given who his lover was. "Says the man who drags me off for a nap nearly every afternoon?"

"Mmm...okay, can I tell you a secret?" Ryder's lips brushed his ear. "He's a little kinky."

It was all he could do not to laugh. Poor Ryder was very serious. "Yes, I know," he replied quietly. "That's what I was getting at. He will probably feel right at home at the men's club, and we need to let him be...himself. Kinky. Submissive, I think."

"I don't have to watch, though, right? That's weird. He's my brother."

He did chuckle that time. "Definitely not. One assumes those things belong behind closed doors."

"You don't want to watch either, right? I mean... I want you to watch *me*. Not another man."

"Oh, no." He took a quick kiss to prove his point. "I have no interest in anyone but you. Watching or otherwise."

"Good." Oh, that little bit of possessiveness felt lovely.

He smiled, kissing Ryder again. "Indeed. You are more than enough for me."

Ryder nodded, kissing him harder. "Want to go...nap?"

"No." His shot Ryder a sly grin. "Now I am going to make you wait until tonight." He expected Roper to be up shortly anyway.

"So mean!" Ryder's face was a study in hunger, in happiness. "I suppose I can live with that..."

"I think we both can. It will make our evening better. Though we might make Roper ill being too...sweet." He didn't care at all. He was just amused by the idea.

"If I had a dime for every time he said I was too sweet..." Ryder kissed the corner of his lips.

"It's why I never mixed the two of you up. Your faces are very similar, but you're really not alike at all."

Ryder beamed at him. "Thank you, Sir. That's important to me."

"I know." He smiled at Ryder. "As I said earlier, you're the right one for me."

"Maybe the only one for you, now?" Ryder flushed dark. "You're the only one for me."

"The only one, now." Tad would be incredibly jealous and incredibly happy for him. "Right, and only."

"Yes, Sir. And only." He got kisses to his knuckles, one at a time.

His phone rang, interrupting them, and really it was just as well because he was about ready to haul Ryder off to the bedroom. He dragged his phone off the coffee table. "It's Victor. Hello, Victor."

"Charles. I was just checking in with you about tomorrow night, and the new sub—"

"Roper," he offered, glad he hadn't put Victor on speaker.

"Yes, Roper. Typically we have an interview with a new sub that might be interested in being paired with a Dom."

"Oh. Hm." That complicated things a bit, but it did make sense. "Well, we can make time for that, I'm sure."

"I'm assuming there's some...awkwardness about this situation?"

He chuckled softly. "You're a perceptive man."

"That's my job. How would you like to address this? A luncheon tomorrow or supper tonight with a small group of us? I know your boy is...tender."

Tender, what a clever way to put it.

"Would dinner tonight give you enough time to properly...evaluate things?" It would change their plans slightly, but sightseeing would be there for another evening.

"I believe so. We will know how to proceed in the best way for all involved, and that's what we need."

"Text me a time and place." He'd sell it to Ryder, and

hopefully Roper would appreciate the care Victor was taking with him.

"I can absolutely do that, yes. How do you feel about Thai?"

"Perfect. Ryder loves it." He looked at Ryder and smiled.

Ryder had a quizzical expression, but he smiled, winked, and nodded.

"Excellent. I'll text you in a bit."

"Sounds good. Thanks, Victor." He ended the call and put his phone down. "Slight change of plans for dinner. Victor has invited us all for Thai with some of the men from the club." He tried to keep his tone very casual. "They want to meet Roper before we go there tomorrow night."

"Oh. Cool. I guess they'd met me at the party, so that makes sense. We both love Thai food, you know?" Ryder nodded and leaned hard, hand on his thigh, petting him. "I'm going to get green curry."

"I may join you." It was Ryder's favorite. He'd always gone for the peanut sauces, but he might just be a convert. "They're probably going to ask him a lot of questions. Some of them will seem very personal, and maybe not what you and I would discuss over dinner, but everyone wants what is best for Roper. Agreed?"

"Yes. And you and I can enjoy our curries and chat." Ryder winked at him. "That's one of my favorite things, Mister Charlie. Chatting with you."

He didn't know when Ryder had come up with Mister Charlie as a nickname. He'd never been called Charlie in his life. Not by anyone, not even friends at school. He'd always been Charles, and he'd even corrected people if they'd shortened it to anything.

He had no intention of correcting Ryder, however. Ryder

used it as a lovely term of endearment, and he accepted it for everything it was.

But he also understood what Ryder was saying. He wanted no part of that conversation.

"We'll talk about our sightseeing plans for tomorrow."

"Yes. And I want to get a special ornament for our tree at home."

Ryder was so good at making a house a home. "Oh, that's a great idea. Do you know what you want to find?"

"No. I want to find it together. We'll know it when we see it."

"Wonderful."

Charles picked up his phone again, then glanced over his shoulder. "You should probably check on Roper, and I need a shower before dinner. Hm?"

"Sure. Do you need me to get anything ironed or polished up for you?"

He was so spoiled, but even so he didn't say no. Ryder needed a little grounding before their evening. "White shirt, gray jacket, black slacks and those shiny shoes you laughed at the first time you saw them."

"I did, but I can see myself in them. I'll get you set after I poke the bear in the butt."

Poor bear. He had no idea whether Roper was ready for this or not. He hoped so, but Victor and his friends seemed to take their lifestyle to a lofty level. It wasn't for him, or for Ryder, but that wasn't what they needed.

Perhaps Roper did.

24

—————

Ryder wasn't as innocent as Roper and Charles thought, and he wasn't dumb either.

He just didn't see any need to dive into pools that he wasn't strong to swim in.

He didn't like big waves or sharks these days, but he loved the hot tub he shared with Charles, and he intended to keep it.

Roper? He needed a more dangerous ocean and a little bit of biting.

"Ry? You okay?"

He blinked, only then noticing the car had stopped at the club and everyone was waiting for him. "Yeah. Yeah, sorry. I was woolgathering."

Charles, who was looking sharp in the jacket he'd made sure was completely lint-free offered him a hand seeming unbothered. "Such an interesting expression."

"Yes, Sir." Oh, his man looked so damn fine, and so did the club, all decked out and classy.

"I've never been here during the holidays; they certainly

spare no expense to welcome members, hm?" Charles pulled his hand through one arm and tucked it close, so possessive. "So no one will wonder who you're with."

"No. Everyone ought to know I'm taken." He thought there was nothing better than being on Charles's arm.

Well...maybe being on Charles's thick cock.

"Mhm." Charles winked at him, and for a second he worried he'd said that out loud. The door was opened for them, as usual, and they were ushered in. "I'm not sure if we're supposed to—"

"Gentlemen." River shook everyone's hands with his usual friendly smile. "Roper, welcome."

"Sir. Pleased." Roper tipped his hat with a smile.

Ryder thought Roper was a little nervous, but he was right here, should Bubba need him.

River gave Roper an approving look and held Roper's hand a little longer than was necessary, covering their grasp with the other hand. "Good boy. Welcome. I have a table for all of us and some people who would like to meet you. Come with me."

Charles winked at him. "We'll sit a while and then perhaps we'll have a dance or move to the bar. Hm?"

"I'd love that. I just need to make sure Roper's safe and happy, and we can do our own thing." It was only fair.

Roper may have been nervous, but he led the way, following River to the table. He and Charles fell in behind them.

"Gentlemen, you remember Charles Martin and Ryder Vales, and this is Roper Vales."

Charles walked around them and pulled out a chair for him. River gestured to a chair for Roper all the way across the table between a couple of men he hadn't met before.

"Roper, this is Master Craig and Master Oliver."

"I'm very pleased to meet y'all, Sirs." Roper nodded, offered them a smile.

"They're handsome," Charles whispered to him.

"Hmm? I guess so." He only had eyes for Charles, who filled up his brain.

Roper was talking quietly with each of the men while River looked on with interest. It was probably just as well that they couldn't hear the conversation.

"Master River, Master Charles, can Ryder and I get you drinks?" Kacey rested steady hands on his shoulders.

"Yes, please. Ryder knows what I want." Charles patted his knee.

"Yes, Sir." He kissed Charles's cheek, then smiled at Kacey. "Merry Christmas, friend. How are you?"

"I'm great. Merry Christmas." Kacey bumped shoulders with him. "You look amazing. You have happy written all over your face."

"I am. I'm having so much fun with him. He makes me stupidly happy." And he was going to do his best to make Charles happy.

"Good deal." Kacey looked over his shoulder. "So...your brother?"

"My twin. Roper. He's a good man." Roper was going to be fine.

"I heard about him. Master River says he's stubborn and naughty. Sounds like the exact opposite of you."

"Well, I'm pretty stubborn, but no one's ever called me naughty, I'm sure."

"I get it all." Kacey chuckled. "Depends on the day."

He glanced back at Roper, who hadn't moved, but was listening intently. "Do you think he'll find a place here? My brother?"

"If he wants a place here, he's already got one. Will he

find the right Dom tonight? No way of knowing, I guess, but he's got people looking out for him. I didn't even know—I mean, he's already light years ahead of where I was when I landed at River's place."

"Yeah?" He didn't want to talk about Roper and kinky stuff together, but he could listen to Kacey talk about River for hours.

"Oh, yeah. All I knew was I was mad and scared and I couldn't ever go home again. I didn't trust anybody."

"Oh, honey. That sucks. I'm so sorry." Awkward. Fuck. "But it did work out for the best."

"You know it. Everything happens for a reason, right?" Kacey smiled and it was hard to believe he was ever in such a bad place.

"That's the rumor. You're led to where you belong." And he belonged with his Mister Charlie, balls to bones.

Kacey waved down the bartender so they could order drinks. "Roper too. He's here now. He's going to okay."

"He is." He nodded to Kacey. "It's good to be home."

They got drinks for their men, though Ryder noted that River's was just a Diet Coke with lime, and headed back to the table, where everyone was laughing.

Roper was smiling and seemed more relaxed. "Hey, Bubba, I was just telling a couple of stories from the road."

"Oh, good Lord and butter." His cheeks heated. "There's sure a lot of those..."

"Tons." Roper waggled his eyebrows.

"Your brother is very entertaining." Craig was laughing along, leaning back in his chair and watching Roper. Oliver was quieter, smiling, and seemed to be watching Roper more than listening.

"He's one hell of a storyteller, yessir. He's a hoot." And he'd better not be embarrassing Charles, dammit.

Kacey set River's drink down and ended up in River's lap. Charles took his drink and patted a seat next to him. As soon as he sat Charles settled an arm around his shoulders. "Thank you."

"You're more than welcome, Sir. You happy?"

"I am. But as much as this is fascinating, I'm not sure our presence is needed at this table."

"No? Would you like to dance? Find a quiet table, all our own?" *Please.*

"I would. Both." Charles leaned over and spoke softly to River for a moment. River gave Charles a smile and a nod before Charles turned back to him. "We've been excused." He got a wide grin.

"Excellent. Night, y'all. Have a good one." He nodded and took Charles's arm.

Charles nodded to Oliver and Craig, then to Roper. "We're not leaving yet. We'll be here if you need us."

"Thank you, sir. I appreciate it very much." Roper gave them both a nod. "Y'all have a good evening."

Charles turned and led him to the small dance floor. "He seems to be fine, but I don't feel ready to leave him on his own yet."

"Sounds perfect." Besides, he wanted to dance with his lover. He moved into Charles's arms, sliding one hand in his.

"I'm glad you agree." Charles curled an arm around his back and danced him in a slow circle. "He's our responsibility for the time being."

Roper had been Ryder's responsibility for their whole lives. He totally understood. "For as long as he needs me."

"Us." Charles pulled him closer, dancing him into the middle of the floor. "As long as he needs us."

"There you go." He could live with that.

In fact, there wasn't much of anything he'd change about his life.

Ryder was finally home.

END

WANT MORE BA & JODI?

Interested in learning more about our East Meets Westerns?

Join BA & Jodi's Newsletter
https://lp.constantcontactpages.com/sl/nzvRTTy

Patreon: https://www.patreon.com/BATortuga
There are lots of tiers to chose from, and also free serial stories.
Discord: https://discord.gg/Vba5P5Qv
BA's Discord server has a channel for BA/Jodi related chat and info.

Hey, Y'all!

We want to thank you for giving Gemini: Ryder a try. We hope you enjoyed the story and want to check out the rest of the series.

If you can spare a few minutes to post a review at the retail website where you made your purchase, we'd very much appreciate it!

Yeehaw and thanks for reading!

BA & Jodi

ABOUT JODI

JODI takes herself way too seriously and has been known to randomly break out in song. Her queer MCs are imperfect but genuine, stubborn but likable, often kinky, and frequently their own worst enemies. They are characters you can't help but fall in love with while they stumble along the path to their happily ever after. For those looking to get on her good side, Jodi's obsessions include nonfat lattes, basketball (go Celtics!), and tequila any way you pour it.

Website: jodipayne.net

Newsletter: https://readerlinks.com/l/2317334

All Jodi's Social Links: linktr.ee/jodipayne

ABOUT BA

Western to the bone and an unrepentant Daddy's Girl, BA Tortuga spends her days with her hounds and her beloved wife, having mother-daughter dates, and eating Mexican food. When she's not doing that, she's writing. She spends her days off watching rodeo, knitting, and surfing Pinterest in the name of research. Following their own personal joys, BA and Julia heard the call of the high desert and they now live in the New Mexico mountains. BA's personal saviors include her wife, her best friends, and coffee. Lots of coffee. Really good coffee.

Having written everything from fist-fighting cowboys to rural single dads to werewolves, BA does her damnedest to tell the stories of her heart, which is committed to giving everyone their happily ever after. With books ranging from heart-warming stories of found families, to rodeo cowboys that are fighting to make a mark, to fiery passionate love affairs, BA refuses to be pigeon-holed by anyone but the voices in her head.

BA loves to talk to her readers and can be found at http:// batortuga.com/ and her newsletter signup link is http://bit. ly/BAJulianews

AVAILABLE FROM JODI & BA

<u>East Meets Westerns</u>

The On the Ranch Series

Tending Tyler

Roped In

Diamonds in the Rough

Outfoxed

The Wrecked Universe

Wrecked

Flying Blind

Special Delivery, A Wrecked Holiday Novel

Seeds and Sunshine

Pickup Man

Cowboy for Sale

The Merry Everything Series

Window Dressing

Cowboy Protection

Cowboys and Cupcakes

Thawed Out

A Present for Parker

The Higher Elevation Series

Heart of a Cowboy

Keeping Promises

Bigger Than Us

Home Free

<u>BDSM/Kink</u>

The Cowboy and the Dom Trilogy

First Rodeo, Book One

Razor's Edge, Book Two

No Ghosts, Book Three

The Soldier and the Angel, a Cowboy and Dom Novel

The Sin Deep Series

(set in The Cowboy and the Dom Universe)

Sin Deep

Trouble with Cowboys

Gemini: Ryder

Gemini: Roper

The Triskelion Series

Breaking the Rules

Making a Mark

Making the Rules

Les's Bar Series

Just Dex

Hide Bound

Wholly Trinity

New Tricks

Lost Boy

The Barn Series

Zeke & Wesley

<u>Other Titles</u>

The Collaborations Series

Refraction

Syncopation

Puzzles Series

Cryptic

Single Titles

Temptation Ranch

Land of Enchantment

Summit Springs Sapphic (F/F) Romance

Christmas Bizarre

Honeymoon in the Cards